James Elgin Wetherell

Later American Poems

James Elgin Wetherell

Later American Poems

ISBN/EAN: 9783744769679

Printed in Europe, USA, Canada, Australia, Japan

Cover: Foto ©Andreas Hilbeck / pixelio.de

More available books at **www.hansebooks.com**

LATER

American Poems

Edited by

J. E. WETHERELL, B.A.

Editor of "Later Canadian Poems."

TORONTO:

THE COPP, CLARK COMPANY, LIMITED

1896.

Preface.

This anthology, as its title suggests, is intended as a companion to the editor's earlier book, "Later Canadian Poems." The scope, however, of this collection of American poems is very much wider. American literature divides itself naturally into two epochs,—the earlier including the great names of Bryant, Whittier, Emerson, Longfellow, Poe, Holmes, Lowell and Whitman,—the later including all the living poets and their deceased contemporaries. This anthology, therefore, embodies a collection of American poems written since about 1860, omitting the work of those poets of the earlier epoch that continued to write after that date.

The selections in this volume are quoted from the works of more than fifty authors. The number might easily have been increased to a hundred, but a manual such as this cannot be exhaustive. All the greatest writers of verse of the present epoch are, it is believed, represented here. Of the minor poets some readers may miss a favorite or two, but a cogent reason could be given for every omission. The present volume is intended mainly as a supplementary reading-book for Canadian High Schools, and that design has influenced the editor not only in his choice of poems but also in determining the limitation in the list of authors.

The editor has taken care to include representations of the work of some writers of exquisite verse at present not

Preface.

widely known in this country. Mr. Sladen's almost exhaustive anthology of "American Poets" published in 1891 (to which the present editor is much indebted) does not contain the names of John B. Tabb, Robert Underwood Johnson, Lizette W. Reese, Gertrude Hall, Harriet Monroe, Bessie Chandler, Stuart Sterne, Elizabeth Akers, Emily Dickenson, Emily Hutchinson, and others included here, who have done remarkable work, or whose poems for the first time have been offered to the public, in very recent years.

In making his selections the editor has attempted to quote poems that adequately display the distinctive characteristics of each author. From the poems themselves, accordingly, the reader must get his estimate of the salient qualities and excellencies of each writer's verse. In the case of living authors, indeed, it might be invidious to undertake a comparison of status or even of style.

The portraits in the book are from photographs furnished by the authors themselves. To Mrs. Lanier's kindness is due the appearance in the volume of the picture of her lamented husband, Sidney Lanier, the greatest poet of the South. For obvious reasons only a few illustrations could appear, and the difficulty of making a selection was increased by the fact that several of the authors preferred to be represented by their poems alone.

Grateful acknowledgments are due to the poets represented in this book for the kind aid they have given the editor in getting the poems together, and for their generous permission to publish.

J. E. W.

iv

Contents.

Contents.

Contents.

Contents.

Contents.

Contents.

Contents.

Contents.

Contents.

EDMUND CLARENCE STEDMAN.

LATER AMERICAN POEMS.

———

Edmund Clarence Stedman.

[Born at Hartford, Connecticut, 1833. Graduated at Yale, 1853.
The author of several volumes of poems and of the well-known
critical works, *Victorian Poets* and *Poets of America*. His latest
work is *A Victorian Anthology*. The poems selected are quoted by
permission of the author and by special arrangement with his publishers, Houghton, Mifflin & Co., Boston.]

——— —◆— ——   ·

The Hand of Lincoln.

Look on this cast, and know the hand
   That bore a nation in its hold ;
From this mute witness understand
   What Lincoln was,—how large of mould

The man who sped the woodman's team,
   And deepest sunk the plowman's share,
And pushed the laden raft astream,
   Of fate before him unaware.

I

B

This was the hand that knew to swing
  The axe—since thus would Freedom train
Her son—and made the forest ring,
  And drove the wedge, and toiled amain.

Firm hand, that loftier office took,
  A conscious leader's will obeyed,
And, when men sought his word and look,
  With steadfast might the gathering swayed.

No courtier's, toying with a sword,
  Nor minstrel's, laid across a lute ;
A chief's, uplifted to the Lord
  When all the kings of earth were mute !

The hand of Anak, sinewed strong,
  The fingers that on greatness clutch,
Yet, lo ! the marks their lines along
  Of one who strove and suffered much.

For here in knotted cord and vein
  I trace the varying chart of years ;
I know the troubled heart, the strain,
  The weight of Atlas—and the tears.

2

Edmund Clarence Stedman.

Again I see the patient brow
   That palm erewhile was wont to press ;
And now 'tis furrowed deep, and now
   Made smooth with hope and tenderness.

For something of a formless grace
   This moulded outline plays about ;
A pitying flame, beyond our trace,
   Breathes like a spirit, in and out,—

The love that cast an aureole
   Round one who, longer to endure,
Called mirth to ease his ceaseless dole,
   Yet kept his nobler purpose sure.

Lo, as I gaze, the statured man,
   Built up from yon large hand, appears :
A type that Nature wills to plan
   But once in all a people's years.

What better than this voiceless cast
   To tell of such a one as he,
Since through its living semblance passed
   The thought that bade a race be free !

Creole Lover's Song.

Night wind, whispering wind,
  Wind of the Carib Sea !
The palms and the still lagoon
Long for thy coming soon ;
But first my lady find :
Hasten, nor look behind—
  To-night Love's herald be !

The feathery bamboo moves,
  The dewy plantains weep ;
From the jasmine-thicket bear
The scents that are swooning there,
And steal from the orange groves
The breath of a thousand loves,
  To bear to her ere she sleep.

And the lone bird's tender song,
  That rings from the ceiba tree ;
The fire-fly's light, and the glow
Of the moon-lit waters low,—
All things that to night belong,
And can do my love no wrong,
  Bear her this hour for me.

Speed thee, wind of the deep,
  For the cyclone comes in wrath !
The distant forests moan ;
Thou hast but an hour thine own—
An hour thy tryst to keep,
Ere the hounds of tempest leap
  And follow upon thy path !

Whisperer, tarry a space !
  She waits for thee in the night ;
She leans from the casement there,
With the star-blooms in her hair,
And a shadow falls like lace
From the fern-tree over her face,
  And over her mantle white.

Spirit of air and fire,
  To-night my herald be !
Tell her I love her well,
And all that I bid thee, tell,
And fold her ever the nigher
With the strength of my soul's desire,
  Wind of the Carib Sea !

The Doorstep.

The conference-meeting through at last,
  We boys around the vestry waited
To see the girls come tripping past,
  Like snow-birds willing to be mated.

Not braver he that leaps the wall
  By level musket-flashes litten,
Than I, who stepped before them all,
  Who longed to see me get the mitten.

But no, she blushed and took my arm !
  We let the old folks have the highway,
And started towards the Maple Farm
  Along a kind of lovers' by-way.

I can't remember what we said,
  'Twas nothing worth a song or story,
Yet that rude path by which we sped
  Seemed all transformed and in a glory.

The snow was crisp beneath our feet,
  The moon was full, the fields were gleaming ;
By hood and tippet sheltered sweet
  Her face with youth and health was beaming.

6

The little hand outside her muff—
  O sculptor, if you could but mould it !—
So lightly touched my jacket-cuff,
  To keep it warm I had to hold it.

To have her with me there alone,—
  'Twas love and fear and triumph blended ;
At last we reached the foot-worn stone
  Where that delicious journey ended.

The old folks, too, were almost home ;
  Her dimpled hand the latches fingered,
We heard the voices nearer come,
  Yet on the doorstep still we lingered.

She shook her ringlets from her hood,
  And with a " Thank you, Ned," dissembled,
But yet I knew she understood
  With what a daring wish I trembled.

A cloud passed kindly overhead,
  The moon was slyly peeping through it,
Yet hid its face, as if it said,
  " Come, now or never ! do it ! *do it !* "

My lips till then had only known
  The kiss of mother and of sister,
But somehow, full upon her own
  Sweet, rosy, darling mouth—I kissed her !

7

Perhaps 'twas boyish love, yet still,
  O listless woman ! weary lover !
To feel once more that fresh, wild thrill,
  I'd give—But who can live youth over ?

Fuit Ilium.

One by one they died,—
  Last of all their race ;
Nothing left but pride,
    Lace, and buckled hose.
Their quietus made,
  On their dwelling-place
Ruthless hands are laid :
    Down the old house goes !

See the ancient manse
  Meet its fate at last !
Time, in his advance,
    Age nor honor knows ;
Axe and broadaxe fall,
  Lopping off the Past :
Hit with bar and maul,
    Down the old house goes !

Edmund Clarence Stedman.

Sevenscore years it stood :
  Yes, they built it well,
Though they built of wood,
    When that house arose.
For its cross-beams square
  Oak and walnut fell ;
Little worse for wear,
    Down the old house goes !

Rending board and plank,
  Men with crowbars ply,
Opening fissures dank,
    Striking deadly blows.
From the gabled roof
  How the shingles fly !
Keep you here aloof,—
    Down the old house goes !

Holding still its place,
  There the chimney stands,
Staunch from top to base,
    Frowning on its foes.
Heave apart the stones,
  Burst its iron bands !
How it shakes and groans !
    Down the old house goes !

Round the mantel-piece
  Glisten Scripture tiles ;
Henceforth they shall cease
      Painting Egypt's woes,
Painting David's fight,
  Fair Bathsheba's smiles,
Blinded Samson's might,—
      Down the old house goes !

On these oaken floors
  High-shoed ladies trod ;
Through those panelled doors
      Trailed their furbelows :
Long their day has ceased ;
  Now, beneath the sod,
With the worms they feast,—
      Down the old house goes !

Many a bride has stood
  In yon spacious room ;
Here her hand was wooed
      Underneath the rose ;
O'er that sill the dead
  Reached the family tomb :
All, that were, have fled,—
      Down the old house goes !

Edmund Clarence Stedman.

Once, in yonder hall,
  Washington, they say,
Led the New-Year's ball,
    Stateliest of beaux.
O that minuet,
  Maids and matrons gay!
Are there such sights yet?
    Down the old house goes!

British troopers came
  Ere another year,
With their coats aflame,
    Mincing on their toes;
Daughters of the house
  Gave them haughty cheer,
Laughed to scorn their vows,—
    Down the old house goes!

Doorway high the box
  In the grass-plot spreads;
It has borne its locks
    Through a thousand snows;
In an evil day,
  From those garden-beds
Now 'tis hacked away,—
    Down the old house goes!

11

Lo ! the sycamores,
  Scathed and scrawny mates,
At the mansion doors
    Shiver, full of woes ;
With its life they grew,
  Guarded well its gates ;
Now their task is through,—
    Down the old house goes !

On this honored site
  Modern trade will build,—
What unseemly fright
    Heaven only knows !
Something peaked and high,
  Smacking of the guild :
Let us heave a sigh,—
    Down the old house goes !

———

The Discoverer.

I have a little kinsman
Whose earthly summers are but three,
And yet a voyager is he
Greater than Drake or Frobisher,
Than all their peers together!
He is a brave discoverer,
And, far beyond the tether
Of them who seek the frozen pole,
Has sailed where the noiseless surges roll.
Ay, he has travelled whither
A winged pilot steered his bark
Through the portals of the dark,
Past hoary Mimir's well and tree,
Across the unknown sea.

Suddenly, in his fair young hour,
Came one who bore a flower,
And laid it in his dimpled hand
With this command :
" Henceforth thou art a rover !
Thou must make a voyage far,
Sail beneath the evening star,

And a wondrous land discover."
—With his sweet smile innocent
 Our little kinsman went.

Since that time no word
From the absent has been heard.
 Who can tell
How he fares, or answer well
What the little one has found
Since he left us, outward bound?
Would that he might return!
Then should we learn
From the pricking of his chart
How the skyey roadways part.
Hush! does not the baby this way bring,
 To lay beside this severed curl,
  Some starry offering
 Of chrysolite or pearl?

 Ah, no! not so!
We may follow on his track,
 But he comes not back.
 And yet I dare aver
He is a brave discoverer
Of climes his elders do not know.
He has more learning than appears

Edmund Clarence Stedman.

On the scroll of twice three thousand years,
More than in the groves is taught,
Or from furthest Indies brought ;
He knows, perchance, how spirits fare,—
What shapes the angels wear,
What is their guise and speech
In those lands beyond our reach,—
    And his eyes behold
Things that shall never, never be to mortal bearers told.

———————

John James Piatt.

[Born at Milton, Indiana, 1835. Poet and journalist. For the last thirteen years (1882-1895) United States Consul at Cork, Ireland. The poems selected are quoted by permission of the author, and by special arrangement with his publishers, Houghton, Mifflin & Co., Boston.]

Apart.

At sea are tossing ships ;
  On shore are dreaming shells,
And the waiting heart and the loving lips,
  Blossoms and bridal bells.

At sea are sails a-gleam ;
  On shore are longing eyes,
And the far horizon's haunting dream
  Of ships that sail the skies.

At sea are masts that rise
  Like spectres from the deep ;
On shore are the ghosts of drowning cries
  That cross the waves of sleep.

17

At sea are wrecks a-strand ;
  On shore are shells that moan,
Old anchors buried in barren sand,
  Sea-mist and dreams alone.

———————

The Buried Ring.

Across the door-step, worn and old,
  The new bride, joyous, pass'd to-day ;
The grey rooms show'd an artful gold,
  All words were light, all faces gay.

Ah, many years have lived and died
  Since she, the other vanish'd one,
Into that door, a timid bride,
  Bore from the outer world the sun.

O lily, with the rose's glow !
  O rose i' the lily's garment clad !—
The rooms were golden long ago,
  All words were blithe, all faces glad.

18

John James Platt.

She wore upon her hand the ring,
  Whose frail and human bond is gone—
A coffin keeps the jealous thing
  Radiant in shut oblivion :

For she, (beloved, who loved so well,)
  In the last tremors of her breath,
Whisper'd of bands impossible—
  " She would not give her ring to Death."

But he, who holds a newer face
  Close to his breast with eager glow,
Has he forgotten her embrace,
  The first shy maiden's, long ago ?

Lo, in a ghostly dream of night,
  A vision, over him she stands,
Her mortal face in heavenlier light,
  With speechless blame but blessing hands !

And, smiling mortal sorrow's pain
  Into immortal peace more deep,
She gives him back her ring again—
  The new bride kisses him from sleep !

William Winter.

[Born at Gloucester, Mass., 1836. Poet and journalist. Dramatic critic of the New York "Tribune." The poems selected are quoted from "The Wanderers" by permission of the author and his publishers, Macmillan & Co.]

My Queen.

He loves not well whose love is bold !
    I would not have thee come too nigh:
The sun's gold would not seem pure gold
    Unless the sun were in the sky :
To take him thence and chain him near
Would make his beauty disappear.

He keeps his state,—do thou keep thine,
    And shine upon me from afar !
So shall I bask in light divine,
    That falls from love's own guiding star ;
So shall thy eminence be high,
And so my passion shall not die.

21

But all my life will reach its hands
  Of lofty longing toward thy face,
And be as one who speechless stands
  In rapture at some perfect grace!
My love, my hope, my all will be
To look to heaven and look at thee !

Thy eyes will be the heavenly lights ;
  Thy voice the gentle summer breeze,
What time it sways, on moonlit nights,
  The murmuring tops of leafy trees ;
And I will touch thy beauteous form
In June's red roses, rich and warm.

But thou thyself shall come not down
  From that pure region far above ;
But keep thy throne and wear thy crown,
  Queen of my heart and queen of love !
A monarch in thy realm complete,
And I a monarch—at thy feet !

Sweet Bells of Stratford.

Sweet bells of Stratford, tolling slow,
In summer gloaming's golden glow,
I hear and feel thy voice divine,
And all my soul responds to thine.

22

William Winter.

As now I hear thee, even so
My Shakespeare heard thee long ago,
When lone by Avon's pensive stream
He wandered in his haunted dream.

Heard thee, and far his fancy sped
Through spectral caverns of the dead,
And sought—and sought in vain—to pierce .
The secret of the universe.

As now thou mournest didst thou mourn
On that sad day when he was borne
Through the long aisle of honeyed limes
To rest beneath the chambered chimes.

He heard thee not, nor cared to hear !
Another voice was in his ear,
And, freed from all the bonds of men,
He knew the awful secret then.

Sweet bells of Stratford, toll, and be
A golden promise unto me
Of that great hour when I shall know
The path whereon his footsteps go !

THOMAS BAILEY ALDRICH

Thomas Bailey Aldrich.

[Born at Portsmouth, N. H., 1836. Poet, novelist, and journalist.
Editor of the " Atlantic Monthly," 1881-1890. The poems quoted
were selected for this anthology by Mr. Aldrich, and are printed by
special permission of Houghton, Mifflin & Co., Boston.]

In Westminster Abbey.

Tread softly here ; the sacredest of tombs
Are those that hold your poets.   Kings and queens
Are facile accidents of Time and Chance ;
Chance sets them on the heights, they climb not there !
But he who from the darkling mass of men
Is on the wing of heavenly thought upbore
To finer ether, and becomes a voice
For all the voiceless, God anointed him !
His name shall be a star, his grave a shrine.

Tread softly here, in silent reverence tread,
Beneath those marble cenotaphs and urns
Lies richer dust than ever nature hid
Packed in the mountain's adamantine heart,
Or slyly wrapt in unsuspecting sand.
The dross men toil for often stains the soul.
How vain and all ignoble seems the greed
To him who stands in this dim cloistered air
With these most sacred ashes at his feet !

This dust was Chaucer, Spenser, Dryden this ;
The spark that once illumed it lingers still.
O, ever-hallowed spot of English earth !
If the unleashed and happy spirit of man
Have option to revisit our dull globe,
What august shades at midnight here convene
In the miraculous sessions of the moon,
When the great pulse of London faintly throbs,
And one by one the stars in heaven pale !

Andromeda.

The smooth-worn coin and threadbare classic phrase
Of Grecian myths that did beguile my youth,
Beguile me not as in the olden days :
I think more grief and beauty dwell with truth.
Andromeda, in fetters by the sea,
Star-pale with anguish till young Perseus came,
Less moves me with her suffering than she,
The slim girl figure fettered to dark shame,
That nightly haunts the park, there, like a shade,
Trailing her wretchedness from street to street.
See where she passes—neither wife nor maid.
How all mere fiction crumbles at her feet !
Here is woe's self, and not the mask of woe :
A legend's shadow shall not move you so !

Outward Bound.

I leave behind me the elm-shadowed square
And carven portals of the silent street,
And wander on with listless, vagrant feet
Through seaward-leading alleys, till the air
Smells of the sea, and straightway then the care
Slips from my heart, and life once more is sweet.
At the lane's ending lie the white-winged fleet.
O restless Fancy, whither wouldst thou fare?
Here are brave pinions that shall take thee far—
Gaunt hulks of Norway ; ships of red Ceylon ;
Slim-masted lovers of the blue Azores !
'Tis but an instant hence to Zanzibar,
Or to the regions of the midnight sun :
Ionian isles are thine, and all the fairy shores !

Identity.

Somewhere—in desolate wind-swept space—
  In Twilight-land—in No-man's land—
Two hurrying Shapes met face to face,
  And bade each other stand.

"And who are you?" cried one, agape,
  Shuddering in the gloaming light.
"I know not," said the Second Shape,
  "I only died last night !"

On an Intaglio Head of Minerva.

Beneath the warrior's helm, behold
  The flowing tresses of the woman !
Minerva, Pallas, what you will—
  A winsome creature, Greek or Roman.

Minerva ? No ! 't is some sly minx
  In cousin's helmet masquerading ;
If not—then Wisdom was a dame
  For sonnets and for serenading !

I thought the goddess cold, austere,
  Not made for love's despairs and blisses :
Did Pallas wear her hair like that ?
  Was Wisdom's mouth so shaped for kisses?

The Nightingale should be her bird,
  And not the Owl, big-eyed and solemn :
How very fresh she looks, and yet
  She's older far than Trajan's Column !

The magic hand that carved this face,
  And set this vine-work round it running,
Perhaps ere mighty Phidias wrought
  Had lost its subtle skill and cunning.

28

Thomas Bailey Aldrich.

Who was he? Was he glad or sad,
  Who knew to carve in such a fashion?
Perchance he graved the dainty head
  For some brown girl that scorned his passion.

Perchance, in some still garden-place,
  Where neither fount nor tree to-day is,
He flung the jewel at the feet
  Of Phryne, or perhaps 't was Laïs.

But he is dust; we may not know
  His happy or unhappy story:
Nameless, and dead these centuries,
  His work outlives him —there's his glory!

Both man and jewel lay in earth
  Beneath a lava-buried city;
The countless summers came and went
  With neither haste, nor hate, nor pity.

Years blotted out the man, but left
  The jewel fresh as any blossom,
Till some Visconti dug it up—
  To rise and fall on Mabel's bosom!

O nameless brother! see how Time
  Your gracious handiwork has guarded:

See how your loving, patient art
    Has come, at last, to be rewarded.

Who would not suffer slights of men,
    And pangs of hopeless passion also,
To have his carven agate-stone
    On such a bosom rise and fall so!

———————

William Dean Howells.

[Born at Martinsville, Ohio, 1837. Poet and novelist. Editor of the " Atlantic Monthly," 1871-1881. The poems selected are quoted with the permission of the author and by special arrangement with his publishers, Houghton, Mifflin & Co., Boston.]

Thanksgiving.

I.

Lord, for the erring thought
Not into evil wrought :
Lord, for the wicked will
Betrayed and baffled still :
For the heart from itself kept,
Our thanksgiving accept.

II.

For ignorant hopes that were
Broken to our blind prayer :
For pain, death, sorrow, sent
Unto our chastisement :
For all loss of seeming good,
Quicken our gratitude.

31

A Springtime.

One knows the spring is coming :
    There are birds ; the fields are green ;
There is balm in the sunlight and moonlight,
    And dew in the twilights between.

But ever there is a silence,
    A rapture great and dumb,
That day when the doubt is ended,
    And at last the spring is come.

Behold the wonder, O silence !
    Strange as if wrought in a night,—
The waited and lingering glory,
    The world-old, fresh delight !

O blossoms that hang like winter,
    Drifted upon the trees,
O birds that sing in the blossoms,
    O blossom-haunting bees,—

O green, green leaves on the branches,
    O shadowy dark below,
O cool of the aisles of orchards,
    Woods that the wild flowers know,—

O air of gold and perfume,
  Wind, breathing sweet and sun,
O sky of perfect azure—
  Day, Heaven and Earth in one !—

Let me draw near thy secret,
  And in thy deep heart see
How fared, in doubt and dreaming,
  The spring that is come in me.

For my soul is held in silence,
  A rapture, great and dumb,—
For the mystery that lingered,
  The glory that is come !

Dead.

I.

Something lies in the room
  Over against my own ;
The windows are lit with a ghastly bloom
  Of candles, burning alone,—
Untrimmed, and all aflare
In the ghastly silence there !

II.

People go by the door,
  Tiptoe, holding their breath,
And hush the talk that they held before,
  Lest they should waken Death,
That is awake all night
There in the candlelight !

III.

The cat upon the stairs
  Watches with flamy eye
For the sleepy one who shall unawares
  Let her go stealing by.
She softly, softly purrs,
And claws at the banisters.

IV.

The bird from out its dream
  Breaks with a sudden song,
That stabs the sense like a sudden scream ;
  The hound the whole night long
Howls to the moonless sky,
So far, and starry, and high.

A Poet.

From wells where Truth in secret lay
He saw the midnight stars by day.

"O marvellous gift!" the many cried,
"O cruel gift!" his voice replied.

The stars were far, and cold, and high,
That glimmered in the noonday sky;

He yearned toward the sun in vain,
That warmed the lives of other men.

The Song the Oriole Sings.

There is a bird that comes and sings
   In the Professor's garden-trees;
Upon the English oak he swings,
   And tilts and tosses in the breeze.

I know his name, I know his note,
   That so with rapture takes my soul;
Like flame the gold beneath his throat,
   His glossy cope is black as coal.

35

O oriole, it is the song
  You sang me from the cottonwood,
Too young to feel that I was young,
  Too glad to guess if life were good.

And while I hark, before my door,
  Adown the dusty Concord road,
The blue Miami flows once more
  As by the cottonwood it flowed.

And on the bank that rises steep,
  And pours a thousand tiny rills,
From death and absence laugh and leap
  My school-mates to their flutter-mills.

The blackbirds jangle in the tops
  Of hoary-antlered sycamores ;
The timorous killdee starts and stops
  Among the drift-wood on the shores.

Below, the bridge—a noonday fear
  Of dust and shadow shot with sun—
Stretches its gloom from pier to pier,
  Far unto alien coasts unknown.

And on those alien coasts, above,
  Where silver ripples break the stream's
Long blue, from some roof-sheltering grove
  A hidden parrot scolds and screams.

Ah, nothing, nothing ! Commonest things :
   A touch, a glimpse, a sound, a breath—
It is a song the oriole sings—
   And all the rest belongs to death.

But oriole, my oriole,
   Were some bright seraph sent from bliss
With songs of heaven to win my soul
   From simple memories such as this,

What could he tell to tempt my ear
   From you ? What high thing could there be,
So tenderly and sweetly dear
   As my lost boyhood is to me ?

———————.   - -

Henry Ames Blood.

[Born at Temple, New Hampshire, 1838. The poem below appeared in "The Century Magazine" of August, 1883. It is quoted with the permission of the author.]

The Rock in the Sea.

They say that yonder rock once towered
   Upon a wide and grassy plain,
Lord of the land, until the sea
   Usurped his green domain :
Yet now remembering the fair scene
   Where once he reigned without endeavor,
The great rock in the ocean stands
   And battles with the waves forever.

How oft, O rock, must visit thee
   Sweet visions of the ancient calm
All amorous with birds and bees,
   And odorous with balm !
Ah me, the terrors of the time
   When the grim, wrinkled sea advances,
And winds and waves, with direful cries
   Arouse thee from thy happy trances !

39

To no soft tryst they waken thee,
    No sunny scene of perfect rest,
But to the raging sea's vanguard
    Thundering against thy breast :
No singing birds are round thee, now,
    But the wild winds, the roaring surges,
And gladly would they hurl thee down
    And mock thee in eternal dirges.

But be it thine to conquer them ;
    And may thy firm-enduring form
Still frown upon the hurricane,
    Still grandly front the storm :
And while the tall ships come and go,
    And come and go the generations,
May thy proud presence yet remain
    A wonder unto all the nations.

Sometime, perchance, O lonely rock,
    Thou mayest regain thine ancient seat,
Mayest see once more the meadow shine,
    And hear the pasture bleat :
But ah, methinks even then thy breast
    Would stir and yearn with fond emotion,
To meet once more in glorious war
    The roaring cohorts of the ocean.

Henry Ames Blood.

Let me, like thee, thou noble rock,
   Pluck honor from the seas of time ;
Where Providence doth place my feet
   There let me stand sublime :
O life, 'tis very sweet to lie
   Upon thy shores without endeavor,
But sweeter far to breast thy storms
   And battle with thy waves forever.

Abram Joseph Ryan.

[Born in Norfolk, Penn., 1839. Died, 1886. Father Ryan's fame rests chiefly on his war poems, of which the one selected is the most celebrated.]

The Conquered Banner.

Furl that Banner, for 'tis weary ;
Round its staff 'tis drooping dreary ;
  Furl it, fold it, it is best ;
For there's not a man to wave it,
And there's not a sword to save it,
And there's not one left to lave it
In the blood which heroes gave it ;
And its foes now scorn and brave it ;
  Furl it, hide it—let it rest.

Take the Banner down ! 'tis tattered ;
Broken is its shaft and shattered ;
And the valiant hosts are scattered
  Over whom it floated high.
Oh ! 'tis hard for us to fold it ;
Hard to think there's none to hold it ;
Hard that those who once unrolled it
  Now must furl it with a sigh.

43

Furl that Banner ! furl it sadly !
Once ten thousand hailed it gladly,
And ten thousand wildly, madly,
　　Swore it should for ever wave ;
Swore that foeman's sword should never
Hearts like theirs entwined dissever,
Till that flag should float for ever
　　O'er their freedom or their grave !

Furl it ! for the hands that grasped it,
And the hearts that fondly clasped it,
　　Cold and dead are lying low ;
And that Banner—it is trailing !
While around it sounds the wailing
　　Of its people in their woe.
For though conquered, they adore it !
Love the cold, dead hands that bore it !
Weep for those who fell before it !
Pardon those who trailed and tore it !
But, oh ! wildly they deplore it,
　　Now who furl and fold it so.

Furl that Banner !　True, it's gory,
Yet 'tis wreathed around with glory,
And 'twill live in song and story,
　　Though its folds are in the dust :

44

Abram Joseph Ryan.

For its fame on brightest pages
Penned by poets and by sages,
Shall go sounding down the ages—
   Furl its folds though now we must.

Furl that Banner, softly, slowly !
Treat it gently—it is holy—
   For it droops above the dead.
Touch it not—unfold it never,
Let it droop then, furled for ever,
   For its people's hopes are dead !

———

Francis Bret Harte.

[Born in Albany, N.Y., 1839. Poet and novelist. United States Consul at Glasgow, 1880-85. Has since lived in England. The poems selected are quoted by special arrangement with Houghton, Mifflin & Co., Boston.]

The Angelus.

Heard at the Mission Dolores, 1868.

Bells of the Past, whose long-forgotten music
  Still fills the wide expanse,
Tingeing the sober twilight of the Present
  With colour of romance.

I hear your call, and see the sun descending
  On rock and wave and sand,
As down the coast the Mission voices blending
  Girdle the heathen land.

Within the circle of your incantation
  No blight nor mildew falls ;
Nor fierce unrest, nor lust, nor low ambition
  Passes those airy walls.

Borne on the swell of your long waves receding,
  I touch the farther Past,—
I see the dying glow of Spanish glory,
  The sunset dream and last !

Before me rise the dome-shaped Mission towers,
  The white Presidio ;
The swart commander in his leathern jerkin,
  The priest in stole of snow.

Once more I see Portala's cross uplifting
  Above the setting sun ;
And past the headland, northward, slowly drifting
  The freighted galleon.

O solemn bells ! whose consecrated masses
  Recall the faith of old,—
O tinkling bells ! that lulled with twilight music
  The spiritual fold !

Your voices break and falter in the darkness,—
  Break, falter, and are still ;
And veiled and mystic, like the Host descending,
  The sun sinks from the hill !

Dickens in Camp.

Above the pines the moon was slowly drifting,
  The river sang below ;
The dim Sierras, far beyond, uplifting
  Their minarets of snow.

Francis Bret Harte.

The roaring camp-fire, with rude humour, painted
  The ruddy tints of health
On haggard face and form that drooped and fainted
  In the fierce race for wealth.

Till one arose, and from his pack's scant treasure
  A hoarded volume drew,
And cards were dropped from hands of listless leisure
  To hear the tale anew ;

And then, while round them shadows gathered faster,
  And as the firelight fell,
He read aloud the book wherein the Master
  Had writ of " Little Nell."

Perhaps 'twas boyish fancy,—for the reader
  Was youngest of them all,—
But, as he read, from clustering pine and cedar
  A silence seemed to fall ;

The fir-trees, gathering closer in the shadows,
  Listened in every spray,
While the whole camp with " Nell" on English meadows
  Wandered, and lost their way.

And so in mountain solitudes—o'ertaken
  As by some spell divine—
Their cares drop from them like the needles shaken
  From out the gusty pine.

Lost is that camp, and wasted all its fire ;
    And he who wrought that spell ?—
Ah, towering pine and stately Kentish spire,
    Ye have one tale to tell !

Lost is that camp ! but let its fragrant story
    Blend with the breath that thrills
With hop-vines' incense all the pensive glory
    That fills the Kentish hills.

And on that grave where English oak and holly
    And laurel wreaths entwine,
Deem it not all a too-presumptuous folly,—
    This spray of Western pine !

———————

Edward Rowland Sill

[Born at Windsor, Conn., 1841. Graduated at Yale, 1861.
Died, 1887. The poems selected are quoted by special arrangement
with Houghton, Mifflin & Co., Boston.]

Opportunity.

This I beheld, or dreamed it in a dream :—
There spread a cloud of dust along a plain ;
And underneath the cloud, or in it, raged
A furious battle, and men yelled, and swords
Shocked upon swords and shields.   A prince's banner
Wavered, then staggered backward, hemmed by foes.
A craven hung along the battle's edge,
And thought, " Had I a sword of keener steel—
That blue blade that the king's son bears,—but this
Blunt thing !—he snapt and flung it from his hand,
And lowering crept away and left the field.
Then came the king's son, wounded, sore bestead,
And weaponless, and saw the broken sword,
Hilt-buried in the dry and trodden sand,
And ran and snatched it, and with battle-shout
Lifted afresh he hewed his enemy down,
And saved a great cause that heroic day.

51

The Fool's Prayer.

The royal feast was done ; the king
    Sought some new sport to banish care,
And to his jester cried : "Sir Fool,
    Kneel now, and make for us a prayer !"

The jester doffed his cap and bells,
    And stood the mocking court before ;
They could not see the bitter smile
    Behind the painted grin he wore.

He bowed his head, and bent his knee
    Upon the monarch's silken stool ;
His pleading voice arose: " O Lord,
    Be merciful to me, a fool !

" No pity, Lord, could change the heart
    From red with wrong to white as wool—
The rod must heal the sin ; but, Lord,
    Be merciful to me, a fool !

" 'Tis not by guilt the onward sweep
    Of truth and right, O Lord, we stay ;
'Tis by our follies that so long
    We hold the earth from heaven away.

Edward Rowland Sill.

"These clumsy feet, still in the mire,
  Go crushing blossoms without end ;
These hard, well-meaning hands we thrust
  Among the heart-strings of a friend.

" The ill-timed truth we might have kept—
  Who knows how sharp it pierced and stung ?
The word we had not sense to say—
  Who knows how grandly it had rung ?

" Our faults no tenderness should ask,
  The chastening stripes must cleanse them all ;
But for our blunders—oh, in shame
  Before the eyes of heaven we fall.

" Earth bears no balsams for mistakes ;
  Men crown the knave, and scourge the tool
That did his will ; but thou, O Lord,
  Be merciful to me, a fool !"

The room was hushed ; in silence rose
  The King, and sought his gardens cool,
And walked apart, and murmured low,
  " Be merciful to me, a fool !"

James Herbert Morse.

[Born at Hubbardston, Mass., 1841. Graduated at Harvard.
The poems selected are quoted by permission of the author.]

The Power of Beauty.

Thou needst not weave nor spin
Nor bring the wheat-sheaves in,
Nor, forth a-field at morn,
At eve bring home the corn,
Nor on a winter's night
Make blaze the faggots bright.

So lithe and delicate—
So slender is thy state,
So pale and pure thy face,
So deer-like in their grace
Thy limbs, that all do vie
To take and charm the eye.

Thus, toiling where thou'rt not
Is but the common lot :—
Three men mayhap alone
By strength may move a stone;
But, toiling near to thee,
One man may work as three.

If thou but bend a smile
To fall on him the while,
Or if one tender glance,—
Though coy and shot askance,—
His eyes discover, then
One man may work as ten.

Men commonly but ask
"When shall I end my task?"
But seeing thee come in
'Tis, "when may I begin?"
Such power does beauty bring
To take from toil its sting.

If then thou'lt do but this—
Fling o'er the work a bliss
From thy mere presence—none
Shall think thou'st nothing done ;
Thou needst not weave nor spin
Nor bring the wheat-sheaves in.

———

James Herbert Morse.

"Like a Star."

No spirit have I, when the moon is full,
  To run to greet it on the round earth's edge ;
  Nor, when the spring has mantled every hedge
  With all the marvel and the miracle
Of blade, and leaf, and blossom, white as wool,
  Am I the first to cry aloud.   All still,
  When others shout, I lie upon the hill,
  Beholding, maniple on maniple,
The ranks unfold,—leaf, blossom, beast, and bird ;
  Yet in my heart a high priest chants his praise,
  Not less devout because it is not heard
Of men who pass me on the public ways.
  I have no song,—no, not a single bar,—
  But my soul, sleepless, gazes like a star.

Labor and Life.

How to labor and find it sweet :
How to get the good red gold
That veinèd hides in the granite fold
 Under our feet—
The good red gold that is bought and sold,
 Raiment to man, and house, and meat !

And how, while delving, to lift the eye
To the far-off mountains of amethyst,
The rounded hills, and the intertwist
 Of waters that lie
Calm in the valleys, or that white mist
 Sailing across a soundless sky.

Joaquin Miller.

(CINCINNATUS HEINE MILLER.)

[Born in Wabash district, Indiana, 1841. Poet and journalist. Lives in California. Was led to adopt his pseudonym from having written in defense of Joaquin Murietta, a Mexican brigand. The poems selected are quoted by permission of the author.]

Columbus.

Behind him lay the gray Azores,
  Behind the Gates of Hercules ;
Before him not the ghost of shores,
  Before him only shoreless seas.
The good mate said : " Now must we pray,
  For, lo ! the very stars are gone.
Brave Admiral, speak ; what shall I say ?"
  " Why say, ' Sail on ! sail on ! and on !'"

" My men grow mutinous day by day ;
  My men grow ghastly wan and weak."
The stout mate thought of home ; a spray
  Of salt wave washed his swarthy cheek,
" What shall I say, brave Admiral, say,
  If we sight naught but seas at dawn ?"
" Why you shall say at break of day,
  ' Sail on ! sail on ! sail on ! and on !'"

They sailed, and sailed, as winds might blow,
  Until at last the blanched mate said:
"Why, now, not even God would know
  Should I and all my men fall dead.
These very winds forget their way,
  For God from these dread seas is gone,
Now speak, brave Admiral, speak and say—"
  He said: "Sail on! sail on! and on!"

They sailed. They sailed. Then spoke the mate:
  "This mad sea shows its teeth to-night;
He curls his lip, he lies in wait,
  With lifted teeth, as if to bite!
Brave Admiral, say but one good word;
  What shall we do when hope is gone?"
The words leapt as a leaping sword:
  "Sail on! sail on! sail on! and on!"

Then pale and worn, he kept his deck,
  And peered through darkness. Ah, that night
Of all dark nights! And then a speck—
  A light! a light! a light! a light!
It grew, a starlit flag unfurled!
  It grew to be Time's burst of dawn,
He gained a world; he gave that world
  Its grandest lesson: "On! and on!"

Dakota.

Against the cold, clear sky a smoke
Curls like some column to its dome.
An axe with far, faint, boyish stroke,
Rings feebly from a snowy home.
"Oh, father, come !   The flame burns low.
We freeze in this vast field of snow."

But far away, and long, and vain,
Two horses plunge with snow to breast.
The weary father drops the rein,—
He rests in the eternal rest ;
And high against the blue profound
A dark bird circles round and round

SIDNEY LANIER.

Sidney Lanier.

[Born at Macon, Georgia, 1842.   Died in 1881.   Poet and critic.
Lecturer on English Literature at Johns Hopkins University, Baltimore, 1879-1881.   His poems were not published in a volume till
1884.   Through the courtesy of Mrs. Lanier and with the kind permission of Charles Scribner's Sons, New York, the poems selected
are reprinted from this volume, "Poems of Sidney Lanier."]

My Springs.

In the heart of the Hills of Life, I know
Two springs that with unbroken flow
Forever pour their lucent streams
Into my soul's far Lake of Dreams.

Not larger than two eyes, they lie
Beneath the many-changing sky
And mirror all of life and time,
—Serene and dainty pantomime.

Shot through with lights of stars and dawns,
And shadowed sweet by ferns and fawns,
—Thus heaven and earth together vie
Their shining depths to sanctify.

63

Always when the large Form of Love
Is hid by storms that rage above,
I gaze in my two springs and see
Love in his very verity.

Always when Faith with stifling stress
Of grief hath died in bitterness,
I gaze in my two springs and see
A Faith that smiles immortally.

Always when Charity and Hope
In darkness bounden, feebly grope,
I gaze in my two springs and see
A Light that sets my captives free.

Always, when Art on perverse wing
Flies where I cannot hear him sing,
I gaze in my two springs and see
A charm that brings him back to me.

When Labor faints, and Glory fails,
And coy Reward in sighs exhales,
I gaze in my two springs and see
Attainment full and heavenly.

O Love, O Wife, thine eyes are they,
—My springs from out whose shining gray
Issue the sweet celestial streams
That feed my life's bright Lake of Dreams.

My Springs.

Oval and large and passion-pure
And gray and wise and honor-sure ;
Soft as a dying violet-breath
Yet calmly unafraid of death ;

Thronged, like two dove-cotes of gray doves,
With wife's and mother's and poor-folk's loves,
And home-loves and high glory-loves
And science-loves and story-loves,

And loves for all that God and man
In art and nature make or plan,
And lady-loves for spidery lace
And broideries and supple grace

And diamonds and the whole sweet round
Of littles that large life compound,
And loves for God and God's bare truth,
And loves for Magdalen and Ruth,

Dear eyes, dear eyes and rare complete—
Being heavenly-sweet and earthly-sweet,
—I marvel that God made you mine,
For when He frowns, 'tis then ye shine !

Song of the Chattahoochee.

Out of the hills of Habersham,
   Down the valleys of Hall,
I hurry amain to reach the plain,
Run the rapid and leap the fall,
Split at the rock and together again,
Accept my bed, or narrow or wide,
And flee from folly on every side
With a lover's pain to attain the plain
      Far from the hills of Habersham,
      Far from the valleys of Hall.

All down the hills of Habersham,
   All through the valleys of Hall,
The rushes cried *Abide, abide,*
The willful waterweeds held me thrall,
The laving laurel turned my tide,
The ferns and the fondling grass said *Stay*
The dewberry dipped for to work delay,
And the little reeds sighed *Abide, abide,*
      Here in the hills of Habersham,
      Here in the valleys of Hall.

66

Sidney Lanier.

High o'er the hills of Habersham,
    Veiling the valleys of Hall,
The hickory told me manifold
Fair tales of shade, the poplar tall
Wrought me her shadowy self to hold,
The chestnut, the oak, the walnut, the pine,
Overleaning, with flickering meaning and sign,
Said, *Pass not, so cold, these manifold*
    Deep shades of the hills of Habersham,
    These glades in the valleys of Hall.

And oft in the hills of Habersham,
    And oft in the valleys of Hall,
The white quartz shone, and the smooth brook-stone
Did bar me of passage with friendly brawl,
And many a luminous jewel lone
—Crystals clear or a-cloud with mist,
Ruby, garnet and amethyst—
Made lures with the lights of streaming stone
    In the clefts of the hills of Habersham,
    In the beds of the valleys of Hall.

But oh, not the hills of Habersham,
    And oh, not the valleys of Hall
Avail: I am fain for to water the plain,
Downward the voices of Duty call -

Downward, to toil and be mixed with the main,
The dry fields burn, and the mills are to turn,
And a myriad flowers mortally yearn,
And the lordly main from beyond the plain
    Calls o'er the hills of Habersham,
    Calls through the valleys of Hall.

The Marshes of Glynn.

Glooms of the live-oaks, beautiful-braided and woven
With intricate shades of the vines that myriad-cloven
  Clamber the forks of the multiform boughs,—
    Emerald twilights,—
    Virginal shy lights,
Wrought of the leaves to allure to the whisper of vows,
When lovers pace timidly down through the green colonnades
Of the dim sweet woods, of the dear dark woods,
  Of the heavenly woods and glades,
That run to the radiant marginal sand-beach within
    The wide sea-marshes of Glynn ;—

Beautiful glooms, soft dusks in the noon-day fire, —
Wild wood privacies, closets of lone desire,

Chamber from chamber parted with wavering arras of
    leaves,—
Cells for the passionate pleasure of prayer to the soul that
    grieves,
Pure with a sense of the passing of saints through the wood,
Cool for the dutiful weighing of ill with good ;—

O braided dusks of the oak and woven shades of the vine,
While the riotous noon-day sun of the June-day long did
    shine
Ye held me fast in your heart and I held you fast in mine :
But now when the noon is no more, and riot is rest,
And the sun is a-wait at the ponderous gate of the West,
And the slant yellow beam down the wood-aisle doth seem
Like a lane into heaven that leads from a dream,—
Aye, now, when my soul all day hath drunken the soul of
    the oak,
And my heart is at ease from men, and the wearisome sound
    of the stroke
  Of the scythe of time, and the trowel of trade is low,
  And belief overmasters doubt, and I know that I know,
  And my spirit is grown to a lordly great compass within,
That the length and the breadth and the sweep of the marshes
    of Glynn
Will work me no fear like the fear they have wrought me of
    yore
When length was fatigue, and when breadth was but bitter-
    ness sore,

And when terror and shrinking and dreary unnamable pain
Drew over me out of the merciless miles of the plain,—

Oh, now, unafraid, I am fain to face
   The vast sweet visage of space.
To the edge of the wood I am drawn, I am drawn,
Where the gray beach glimmering runs as a belt of the dawn,
   For a mete and a mark
      To the forest dark :—
        So :
Affable live-oak, leaning low,—
Thus—with your favor—soft, with a reverent hand,
(Not lightly touching your person, Lord of the land !)
Bending your beauty aside, with a step I stand
On the firm-packed sand,
       Free
By a world of marsh that borders a world of sea.

Sinuous southward and sinuous northward the shimmering
   band
Of the sand-beach fastens the fringe of the marsh to the
   folds of the land.
Inward and outward to northward and southward the beach
   lines linger and curl
As a silver-wrought garment that clings to and follows the
   firm sweet limbs of a girl.
Vanishing, swerving, evermore curving again into sight,

Softly the sand-beach wavers away to a dim grey looping of
   light.
And what if behind me to westward the wall of the woods
   stands high ?
The world lies east : how ample, the marsh and the sea and
   the sky !
A league and a league of marsh-grass, waist-high, broad in
   the blade,
Green, and all of a height, and unflecked with a light or a
   shade,
Stretch leisurely off, in a pleasant plain,
To the terminal blue of the main.

Oh, what is abroad in the marsh and the terminal sea ?
   Somehow my soul seems suddenly free
From the weighing of fate and the sad discussion of sin,
By the length and the breadth and the sweep of the marshes
   of Glynn.

Ye marshes, how candid and simple and nothing-withholding
   and free
Ye publish yourselves to the sky and offer yourselves to the
   sea !
Tolerant plains, that suffer the sea and the rains and the sun,
Ye spread and span like the catholic man who hath mightily
   won
God out of knowledge and good out of infinite pain
And sight out of blindness and purity out of a stain.

As the marsh-hen secretly builds on the watery sod,

Behold I will build me a nest on the greatness of God :

I will fly in the greatness of God as the marsh-hen flies

In the freedom that fills all the space 'twixt the marsh and
the skies :

By so many roots as the marsh-grass sends in the sod

I will heartily lay me a-hold on the greatness of God :

Oh, like to the greatness of God is the greatness within

The range of the marshes, the liberal marshes of Glynn.

And the sea lends large, as the marsh : lo, out of his plenty
the sea

Pours fast : full soon the time of the flood-tide must be :

Look how the grace of the sea doth go

About and about through the intricate channels that flow

Here and there,

Everywhere,

Till his waters have flooded the uttermost creeks and the
low-lying lanes,

And the marsh is meshed with a million veins,

That like as with rosy and silvery essences flow

  In the rose-and-silver evening glow.

Farewell, my lord Sun !

The creeks overflow : a thousand rivulets run

Twixt the roots of the sod ; the blades of the marsh-grass
stir ;

Passeth a hurrying sound of wings that westward whirr ;

Passeth, and all is still ; and the currents cease to run :
And the sea and the marsh are one.

How still the plains of the waters be !
The tide is in his ecstasy.
The tide is at his highest height ·
         And it is night.

And now from the Vast of the Lord will the waters of sleep
Roll in on the souls of men,
But who will reveal to our waking ken
The forms that swim and the shapes that creep
         Under the waters of sleep?
And I would I could know what swimmeth below when the
   tide comes in
On the length and the breadth of the marvellous marshes of
   Glynn.

———————

Richard Watson Gilder.

[Born at Bordentown, New Jersey, 1844. Poet and editor. Since 1881, editor-in-chief of "The Century" magazine. The poems selected are reprinted from "Five Books of Song" through the kind permission of The Century Co., New York.]

A Woman's Thought.

I am a woman—therefore I may not
Call to him, cry to him,
Fly to him,
Bid him delay not !

Then when he comes to me, I must sit quiet ;
Still as a stone—
All silent and cold.
If my heart riot—
Crush and defy it !
Should I grow bold,
Say one dear thing to him,
All my life fling to him,
Cling to him—
What to atone

Is enough for my sinning !
This were the cost to me,
This were my winning—
That he were lost to me.

Not as a lover
At last if he part from me,
Tearing my heart from me,
Hurt beyond cure—
Calm and demure
Then must I hold me,
In myself fold me,
Lest he discover ;
Showing no sign to him
By look of mine to him
What he has been to me—
How my heart turns to him,
Follows him, yearns to him,
Prays him to love me.

Pity me, lean to me,
Thou God above me !

————————

The Sower.

I.

A Sower went forth to sow;
His eyes were dark with woe;
He crushed the flowers beneath his feet,
Nor smelt the perfume, warm and sweet,
That prayed for pity everywhere.
He came to a field that was harried
By iron, and to heaven laid bare;
He shook the seed that he carried
O'er that brown and bladeless place.
He shook it, as God shakes hail
Over a doomed land,
When lightnings interlace
The sky and the earth, and his wand
Of love is a thunder-flail.
Thus did that Sower sow;
His seed was human blood,
And tears of women and men.
And I, who near him stood,
Said: When the crop comes, then
There will be sobbing and sighing,
Weeping and wailing and crying,
Flame, and ashes, and woe.

II.

It was an autumn day
When next I went that way.
And what, think you, did I see,
What was it that I heard,
What music was in the air?
The song of a sweet-voiced bird?
Nay—but the songs of many,
Thrilled through with praise and prayer
Of all those voices not any
Were sad of memory;
But a sea of sunlight flowed,
A golden harvest glowed,
And I said : Thou only art wise,
God of the earth and skies !
And I praise thee, again and again,
For the Sower whose name is Pain.

"My Love for Thee Doth March Like Armed Men."

My love for thee doth march like arméd men,
  Against a queenly city they would take.
  Along the army's front its banners shake ;
  Across the mountain and the sun-smit plain

It steadfast sweeps as sweeps the steadfast rain ;
  And now the trumpet makes the still air quake,
  And now the thundering cannon doth awake
  Echo on echo, echoing loud again.
But, lo ! the conquest higher than bard e'er sung :
  Instead of answering cannon, proud surrender !
  Joyful the iron gates are open flung
And, for the conqueror, welcome gay and tender !
  Oh, bright the invader's path with tribute flowers,
  While comrade flags flame forth on wall and towers !

At Niagara.

I.

There at the chasm's edge behold her lean
Trembling as, 'neath the charm,
A wild bird lifts no wing to 'scape from harm ;
Her very soul drawn to the glittering, green,
Smooth, lustrous, awful, lovely curve of peril ;
While far below the bending sea of beryl
Thunder and tumult—whence a billowy spray
Enclouds the day.

II.

What dream is hers? No dream hath wrought that spell
The long waves rise and sink ;
Pity that virgin soul on passion's brink,
Confronting Fate,—swift, unescapable,—
Fate, which of nature is the intent and core,
And dark and strong as the steep river's pour,
Cruel as love, and wild as love's first kiss !
Ah, God ! the abyss !

"Great Nature Is An Army Gay."

Great nature is an army gay,
Resistless marching on its way ;
I hear the bugles clear and sweet,
I hear the tread of million feet.

   Across the plain I see it pour ;
It tramples down the waving grass ;
Within the echoing mountain pass
I hear a thousand cannon roar.

   It swarms within my garden gate ;
My deepest well it drinketh dry.
It doth not rest ; it doth not wait :

Richard Watson Gilder.

By night and day it sweepeth by ;
Ceaseless it marches by my door ;
It heeds me not, though I implore.
I know not whence it comes, nor where
It goes.   For me it doth not care—
Whether I starve, or eat, or sleep,
Or live, or die, or sing, or weep.
And now the banners all are bright,
Now torn and blackened by the fight.
Sometimes its laughter shakes the sky,
Sometimes the groans of those who die.
Still through the night and through the livelong day
The infinite army marches on its remorseless way.

———— - — ~ -

MAURICE THOMPSON.

Maurice Thompson.

[Born at Fairfield, Indiana, 1844. The poems selected are quoted by permission of the author and by special arrangement with his publishers, Houghton, Mifflin & Co., Boston.]

In the Haunts of Bream and Bass.

I.

Dreams come true and everything
Is fresh and lusty in the spring.

In groves, that smell like ambergris,
Wind-songs, bird-songs never cease.

Go with me down by the stream,
Haunt of bass and purple bream ;

Feel the pleasure, keen and sweet,
When the cool waves lap your feet ;

Catch the breath of moss and mould,
Hear the grosbeak's whistle bold ;

See the heron all alone
Mid-stream on a slippery stone,

83

Or, on some decaying log,
Spearing snail or water-frog,

Whilst the sprawling turtles swim
In the eddies cool and dim !

II.

The busy nuthatch climbs his tree,
Around the great bole spirally,

Peeping into wrinkles gray,
Under ruffled lichens gay,

Lazily piping one sharp note
From his silver-mailéd throat ;

And down the wind the catbird's song
A slender medley trails along.

Here a grackle chirping low,
There a crested vireo ;

Every tongue of Nature sings,
The air is palpitant with wings !

Halcyon prophecies come to pass
In the haunts of bream and bass.

Maurice Thompson.

III.

Bubble, bubble flows the stream,
Like an old tune through a dream.

Now I cast my silken line ;
See the gay lure spin and shine—

While, with delicate touch, I feel
The gentle pulses of the reel.

Halcyon laughs and cuckoo cries,
Through its leaves the plane-tree sighs.

Bubble, bubble flows the stream,
Here a glow and there a gleam,

Coolness all about me creeping,
Fragrance all my senses steeping,

Spicewood, sweetgum, sassafras,
Calamus and water-grass,

Giving up their pungent smells
Drawn from Nature's secret wells ;

On the cool breath of the morn
Fragrance of the cockspur thorn.

IV.

I see the morning-glory's curl,
The curious star-flower's pointed whorl.

Here the woodpecker, rap-a-tap !
See him with his cardinal's cap !

And the querulous, leering jay,
How he clamors for a fray !

Patiently I draw and cast,
Keenly expectant, till, at last,

Comes a flash, down in the stream,
Never made by perch or bream,

Then a mighty weight I feel,
Sings the line and whirs the reel !

V.

Out of a giant tulip-tree,
A great gay blossom falls on me ;

Old gold and fire its petals are,
It flashes like a falling star.

A big blue heron flying by
Looks at me with a greedy eye.

Maurice Thompson.

I see a stripéd squirrel shoot
Into a hollow maple-root ;

A bumble-bee, with mail all rust,
His thighs puffed out with anther-dust,

Clasps a shrinking bloom about,
And draws her amber sweetness out.

Bubble, bubble flows the stream,
Like an old tune through a dream !

A white-faced hornet hurtles by,
Lags a turquoise butterfly,

One intent on prey and treasure,
One afloat on tides of pleasure !

Sunshine arrows, swift and keen,
Pierce the maple's helmet green.

VI.

I follow where my victim leads,
Through tangles of rank water-weeds,

O'er stone and root and knotty log,
And faithless bits of reedy bog.

87

I wonder will he ever stop?
The reel hums like a humming top !

A thin sandpiper, wild with fright,
Goes into ecstasies of flight,

Whilst I, all flushed and breathless, tear
Through lady-fern and maiden's-hair,

And in my straining fingers feel
The throbbing of the rod and reel !

Bubble, bubble flows the stream,
Like an old tune through a dream !

VII.

At last he tires, I reel him in ;
I see the glint of scale and fin.

I lower rod—I shorten line
And safely land him ; he is mine !

The belted halcyon laughs, the wren
Comes twittering from its brushy den,

The turtle sprawls upon his log,
I hear the booming of a frog.

Maurice Thompson.

Liquidamber's keen perfume,
Sweet-punk, calamus, tulip-bloom,

Glimpses of a cloudless sky
Soothe me as I resting lie.

Bubble, bubble flows the stream,
Like low music through a dream.

Farewell.

Farewell!   It is no sorrowful word,
　　It has never had a pang for me.
Sweet as the last song of a bird,
　　Soft as a wind-swell from the sea,
　　　　　The word Farewell.

I part with you as oft before
　　I've parted with dear friends and sweet,
And now I shake (forevermore)
　　Your memory's gold-dust from my feet.
　　　　　Farewell! farewell!

There's the whole crowd, hearty an' proud.
Hey ! boys, say ! can't you glance up this way ?
Here's an old comrade, crippled now, an' gray !
This is too much.   Girl, throw me my crutch !
I can see—I can walk—I can march—I could fly !
No, I *won't* sit still an' see the boys march by !

Oh !—I fall and I flinch ; I can't go an inch !
No use to flutter ; no use to try.
Where's my strength ?   Hunt down at the front ;
There's where I left it.   No need to sigh ;
All the milk's spilt ; there's no use to cry.
Plague o' these tears, and the moans in my ears !
Part of a war is to suffer and to die.
I must sit still, and let the drums march by.

Part of a war is to suffer and to die—
Suffer and to die—suffer and to—   Why,
Of all the crowd I just yelled at so loud,
There's hardly a one but is killed, dead, and gone !
All the old regiment, excepting only I,
Marched out of sight in the country of the night.
That was a spectre band marched past so grand.
All the old boys are a-tenting in the sky.
Sarah, Sarah, Sarah. hear the drums moan by !

Autumn Days.

Yellow, mellow, ripened days,
 Sheltered in a golden coating ;
O'er the dreamy, listless haze,
 White and dainty cloudlets floating ;
Winking at the blushing trees,
 And the sombre, furrowed fallow ;
Smiling at the airy ease
 Of the southward flying swallow :
Sweet and smiling are thy ways,
Beauteous, golden Autumn days !

Shivering, quivering, tearful days,
 Fretfully and sadly weeping ;
Dreading still, with anxious gaze,
 Icy fetters round thee creeping ;
O'er the cheerless, withered plain,
 Wofully and hoarsely calling ;
Peking hail and drenching rain
 On thy scanty vestments falling ;
Sad and mournful are thy ways,
Grieving, wailing Autumn days !

John B. Tabb.

[Born at "The Forest," Amelia County, Virginia, 1845. Became a priest of the Catholic Church in 1884. For many years a teacher of English in St. Charles College, Ellicott City, Maryland. The poems selected are quoted by permission of the author.]

The Swallow.

Skim o'er the tide,
   And from thy pinions fling
The sparkling water-drops,
   Sweet child of spring !
Bathe in the dying sunshine warm and bright,
Till ebbs the last receding wave of light.

Swift glides the hour,
   But what its flight to thee ?
Thine own is fleeter far ;
   E'en now to me
Thou seem'st upon futurity anon
To beckon thence the tardy present on.

The eye in vain
   Pursues, with subtle glance,
Thy dim, delirious course
   Through heaven's expanse :
Vanished thy form upon the wings of thought,
Ere yet its place the lagging vision caught.

Again thou'rt here,
   A slanting arrow sent
From yon fair-tinted bow,
   In promise bent ;
As when, erewhile, the gentle bird of love
Poised her white wing the new-born land above.

A seeming shade,
   Scarce palpable in form,
Yet thine, alas, the change
   Of calm and storm !
The veering passions of my stronger soul
Alike the throbbings of thy heart control.

For day is done,
   And cloyed of long delight,
Like me thou welcomest
   The sober night ;
Like me, aweary, sinkest on that breast,
That woos all nature to her silent rest.

John B. Tabb.

The Playmate.

Who are thy playmates, boy?
" My favourite is Joy,
Who brings with him his sister, Peace, to stay
    The livelong day.
    I love them both, but he
        Is most to me."

And where thy playmates now,
O man of sober brow?
"Alas! dear Joy, the merriest, is dead.
    But I have wed
    Peace, and our babe, a boy,
        New-born, is Joy."

———————

Edgar Fawcett.

[Born in New York City, 1847. Poet, essayist and novelist.
The poems selected are quoted by permission of the author and by
special arrangement with his publishers, Houghton, Mifflin & Co.,
Boston.]

Other Worlds.

I sometimes muse, when my adventurous gaze
  Has roamed the starry arches of the night,
    That were I dowered with strong angelic sight,
All would look changed in those pale heavenly ways.
What wheeling worlds my vision would amaze !
  What chasms of gloom would thrill me and affright !
    What rhythmic equipoise would rouse delight !
What moons would beam on me, what suns would blaze !

Then through my awed soul sweeps the larger thought
  Of how creation's edict may have set
    Vast human multitudes on those far spheres
With towering passions to which mine mean naught,
  With majesties of happiness, or yet
    With agonies of unconjectured tears !

99

Indian Summer.

Dulled to a drowsy fire, one hardly sees
   The sun in heaven, where this broad smoky round
   Lies ever brooding at the horizon's bound ;
And through the gaunt knolls, on monotonous leas,
Or through the damp wood's troops of naked trees,
   Rustling the brittle ruin along their ground,
   Like sighs from souls of perished hours, resound
The melancholy melodies of the breeze !

So ghostly and strange a look the blurred world wears,
Viewed from the flowerless garden's dreary squares,
   That now, while these weird vaporous days exist,
It would not seem a marvel if where we walk,
We met, dim-glimmering on its thorny stalk,
   Some pale intangible rose with leaves of mist !

To an Oriole.

How falls it, oriole, thou hast come to fly
In tropic splendor through our northern sky?

At some glad moment was it nature's choice
To dower a scrap of sunset with a voice?

Or did some orange tulip, flaked with black,
In some forgotten garden, ages back,

Yearning toward heaven until its wish was heard
Desire unspeakably to be a bird?

———————

Gold.

No spirit of air am I, but one whose birth
Was deep in mouldy darkness of mid-earth.

Yet where my yellow raiments choose to shine,
What power is more magnificent than mine?

In hall or hut, in highway or in street,
Obedient millions grovel at my feet.

The loftiest pride to me its tribute brings ;
I gain the lowly vassalage of kings !

How many a time have I made honor yield
To me its mighty and immaculate shield ?

How often has virtue, at my potent name,
Robed her chaste majesty in scarlet shame ?

How often has burning love, within some breast,
Frozen to treachery at my cold behest ?

Yet ceaselessly my triumph has been blent
With pangs of overmastering discontent ?

For always there are certain souls that hear
My stealthy whispers with indifferent ear.

Pure souls that deem my smile's most blind excess,
For all its lavish radiance, valueless !

Rare souls, from my imperious guidance free,
Who know me for the slave that I should be !

Grand souls, that from my counsels would dissent,
Though each were tempted with a continent !

Ivy.

Ill canst thou bide in alien lands like these,
  Whose home lies over seas,
Among manorial halls, parks wide and fair,
  Churches antique, and where
Long hedges flower in May, and one can hark
To carollings from old England's lovely lark !

Ill canst thou bide where memories are so brief,
  Thou that hast bathed thy leaf
Deep in the shadowy past, and know strange things
  Of crumbled queens and kings ;
Thou whose dead kindred, in years half forgot,
Robed the grey battlements of proud Camelot !

Through all thy fibre's intricate expanse
  Hast thou breathed sweet romance ;
Ladies that long are dust thou hast beheld
  Through dreamy days of eld ;
Watched in broad castle-courts the merry light
Bathe gaudy banneret and resplendent knight.

And thou hast seen, on ancient lordly lawns,
  The timorous dappled fawns ;
Heard pensive pages with their suave lutes play

Some low Provençal lay ;
Marked beauteous dames through arrased chambers glide,
With lazy and graceful stag-hounds at their side.

And thou hast gazed on splendid cavalcades
   Of nobles, matrons, maids,
Winding from castle gates on breezy morns,
    With golden peals of horns,
In velvet and brocade, in plumes and silk,
With falcons, and with palfrey white as milk.

Through convent-casements thou hast peered, and there
   Viewed the meek nun at prayer ;
Seen, through rich panes dyed purple, gold and rose,
   Monks read old folios ;
On abbey-walls heard wild laughs thrill thy vine
When the fat tonsured priests quaffed ruby wine.

O ivy, having lived in times like these,
   Here art thou ill at ease ;
For thou art one with ages passed away,
   We are of yesterday ;
Short retrospect, slight ancestry is ours,
But thy dark leaves clothe history's haughty towers !

John Vance Cheney.

[Born at Groveland, New York, 1848. Librarian of the New-
berry Library, Chicago. The poems selected are quoted by permission of the author.]

To a Humming-Bird.

Voyager on golden air,
Type of all that's fleet and fair,
    Incarnate gem,
    Live diadem,
Bird-beam of the summer day,—
Whither on your sunny way?

Loveliest of all lovely things,
Roses open to your wings;
    Each gentle breast
    Would give you rest;
Stay, forget lost paradise,
Star-bird fallen from happy skies.

105

Vanished ! earth is not his home ;
Onward, onward, must he roam,
Swift passion-thought,
In rapture wrought,
Issue of the soul's desire,
Plumed with beauty and with fire.

———

The Beeches Brighten for Young May.

The beeches brighten for young May,
And young grass shines along her way ;
Joy bares for her his sunny head,
Leaned over brook and blossom-bed ;
The smell of Spring fills all the air,
And wooing birds make music there.
Though nought of sound or sight does grieve,
From quiring morn to quiet eve,
My crowding thoughts are forward cast :
This loveliness—it cannot last.
The merry field, the ringing bough,
Will silent be as voiceful now ;

Chill, warning winds will hither roam,
The Summer's children hasten home :
That blue solicitude of sky
Bent over beauty doomed to die,
Ere long will, pitying, witness here,
The yielded glory of the year.

"I Need Not Hear."

I need not hear each night-wind loud
 Go moaning down the wold,
I need not lift each bleachen shroud
 From bodies white and cold.

Call not, O naked, wailing Fall,
 O man's unhappy race !
One drifting leaflet tells me all,
 'Tis all in one pale face.

Eugene Field.

[Born in St. Louis, Missouri, 1850. Died, 1895. Poet and journalist. The poems selected are quoted by the author's permission, obtained a few months before his death.]

The Dreams.

Two dreams came down to earth one night,
    From the realm of mist and dew;
One was a dream of the old, old days,
    And one was a dream of the new.

One was a dream of a shady lane
    That led to the pickerel pond,
Where the willows and rushes bowed themselves
    To the brown old hills beyond.

And the people that peopled the old-time dream
    Were pleasant and fair to see.
And the dreamer he walked with them again,
    As often of old walked he.

Oh, cool was the wind in the shady lane
    That tangled his curly hair !
Oh, sweet was the music the robins made
    To the springtime everywhere !

Was it the dew the dream had brought
  From yonder midnight skies,
Or was it tears from the dear dead years
  That lay in the dreamer's eyes?

The other dream ran fast and free,
  As the moon benignly shed
Her golden grace on the smiling face
  In the little trundle bed.

For 'twas a dream of times to come—
  Of the glorious noon of day—
Of the summer that follows the ceaseless spring
  When the child is done with play.

And 'twas a dream of the busy world,
  Where valorous deeds are done ;
Of battles fought in the cause of right,
  And of victories nobly won.

It breathed no breath of the dear old home,
  And the quiet joys of youth ;
It gave no glimpse of the good old friends
  Or the old-time faith and truth.

Eugene Field.

But 'twas a dream of youthful hopes,
  And fast and free it ran,
And it told to a little sleeping child,
  Of a boy become a man !

These were the dreams that came one night ;
  To earth from yonder sky ;
These were the dreams two dreamers dreamed—
  My little boy and I.

And in our hearts my boy and I
  Were glad that it was so ;
He loved to dream of days to come,
  And I of long ago.

So from our dreams my boy and I
  Unwillingly awoke,
But neither of his precious dream
  Unto the other spoke.

Yet of the love we bore those dreams
  Gave each his tender sign :
For there was triumph in his eyes—
  And there were tears in mine !

The Humming Top.

The top it hummeth a sweet, sweet song
  To my dear little boy at play—
Merrily singeth all day long,
    As it spinneth and spinneth away.
        And my dear little boy,
        He laugheth with joy
When he heareth the tuneful tone
        Of that busy thing
        That loveth to sing
The song that is all its own.

Hold fast the string and wind it tight,
  That the song be loud and clear ;
Now hurl the top with all your might
  Upon the banquette here ;
        And straight from the string,
        The joyous thing
Boundeth and spinneth along,
        And it whirrs and it chirrs,
        And it birrs and it purrs,
Ever its pretty song.

Will ever my dear little boy grow old,
   As some have grown before ?
Will ever his heart feel faint and cold,
   When he heareth the songs of yore?
      Will ever this toy
      Of my dear little boy,
When the years have worn away,
     Sing sad and low
     Of the long ago,
As it singeth to me to-day ?

Shuffle-Shoon and Amber-Locks.

Shuffle-Shoon and Amber-Locks
Sit together, building blocks ;
   Shuffle-Shoon is old and gray,
    Amber-Locks a little child,
  But together at their play
    Age and Youth are reconciled,
And with sympathetic glee
Build their castles fair to see.

I

"When I grow to be a man"
(So the wee one's prattle ran),
   "I shall build a castle so—
      With a gateway broad and grand;
   Here a pretty vine shall grow,
      There a soldier guard shall stand;
And the tower shall be so high,
Folks will wonder, by and by!"

Shuffle-Shoon quoth : "Yes, I know;
Thus I builded long ago!
   Here a gate and there a wall,
      Here a window, there a door;
   Here a steeple wondrous tall
      Riseth ever more and more!
But the years have levelled low
What I builded long ago!"

So they gossip at their play,
Heedless of the fleeting day;
   One speaks of the Long Ago
      Where his dead hopes buried lie;
   One with chubby cheeks aglow
      Prattleth of the By and By;
Side by side, they build their blocks—
Shuffle-Shoon and Amber-Locks.

Swing High and Swing Low.

Swing high and swing low
While the breezes they blow—
It's off for a sailor thy father would go ;
And it's here in the harbor, in sight of the sea,
He hath left his wee babe with my song and with me.
    " *Swing high and swing low*
        While the breezes they blow!"

Swing high and swing low
While the breezes they blow—
It's oh for the waiting as weary days go !
And it's oh for the heartache that smiteth me when
I sing my song over and over again :
    " *Swing high and swing low*
        While the breezes they blow!"

"Swing high and swing low "—
    The sea singeth so,
And it waileth anon in its ebb and its flow ;
And a sleeper sleeps on to that song of the sea
Nor recketh he ever of mine or of me !
    " *Swing high and swing low*
        While the breezes they blow—
        'T was all for a sailor thy father would go."

Arlo Bates.

[Born at East Machias, Maine, 1850. Graduated at Bowdoin College, 1876. The poems selected are quoted by permission of the author. The Sonnet is the poet's own favorite from "Sonnets in Shadow."]

" We Must be Nobler."

We must be nobler for our dead, be sure,
   Than for the quick.   We might their living eyes
   Deceive with gloss of seeming ; but all lies
Were vain to cheat a prescience spirit-pure.

Our soul's true worth and aim, however poor,
   They see who watch us from some deathless skies
   With glance death-quickened.   That no sad surprise
Sting them in seeing, be ours to secure.

Living, our loved ones make us what they dream ;
   Dead, if they see, they know us as we are ;
Henceforward we must be, not merely seem.

Bitterer woe than death it were by far
   To fail their hopes who love us to redeem ;
Loss were thrice loss that thus their faith should mar.

117

A Shadow Boat.

Under my keel another boat
Sails as I sail, floats as I float ;
Silent and dim and mystic still,
It steals through that weird nether-world,
Mocking my power, though at my will
The foam before its prow is curled,
Or calm it lies, with canvas furled.

Vainly I peer, and fain would see
What phantom in that boat may be ;
Yet half I dread, lest I with ruth
Some ghost of my dead past divine,
Some gracious shape of my lost youth,
Whose deathless eyes once fixed on mine
Would draw me downward through the brine!

Robert Underwood Johnson.

[Born in Washington, D.C., 1853. Author of "The Winter Hour and Other Poems," published by The Century Co., New York (1892). Since 1873 connected with the editorial department of "The Century," and since 1881 its associate editor. The poems are quoted by permission of the author.]

Hearth-Song.

When November's night comes down
With a dark and sudden frown,
Like belated traveler chill
Hurrying o'er the tawny hill,—
  Higher, higher
Heap the pine-cones in a pyre !
Where's a warmer friend than fire?

Song's but solace for a day ;
Wine's a traitor not to trust ;
Love's a kiss and then away ;
Time's a peddler deals in dust.
  Higher, higher
Pile the driftwood in a pyre !
Where's a firmer friend than fire ?

Knowledge was but born to-night ;
Wisdom's to be born to-morrow ;
One more log—and banish sorrow,
One more branch—the world is bright.
          Higher, higher
Crown with balsam-boughs the pyre !
Where's an older friend than fire?

Love in the Calendar.

When chinks in April's windy dome
     Let through a day of June,
And foot and thought incline to roam,
     And every sound's a tune ;
When Nature fills a fuller cup,
     And hides with green the gray,—
Then, lover, pluck your courage up,
     To try your fate in May.

Though proud she was as sunset clad
     In Autumn's fruity shades,
Love too is proud, and brings (gay lad !)
     Humility to maids.
Scorn not from Nature's mood to learn,
     Take counsel of the day :
Since haughty skies to tender turn,
     Go try your fate in May.

Though cold she seemed as pearly light
 Adown December eves,
And stern as night when March winds smite
 The beech's lingering leaves ;
Yet Love hath seasons like the year,
 And grave will turn to gay,—
Then, lover, harken not to fear,
 But try your fate in May.

And you whose art it is to hide
 The constant love you feel :
Beware, lest overmuch of pride
 Your happiness shall steal.
No longer pout, for May is here,
 And hearts will have their way ;
Love's in the calendar, my dear,
 So yield to fate—and May !

October.

Soft days whose silver moments keep
The constant promise of the morn,
When tired equinoctials sleep,
And wintry winds are yet unborn :
What one of all the twelve more dear—
Thou truce and Sabbath of the year ?

More restful art thou than the May,
And if less hope be in thy hand,
Some cares 'twere grief to understand
Thou hid'st, as is the mother's way,
With mists and lights of fairy-land
Set on the borders of the day.

And best of all thou dost beguile
With color,-- friendliest thought of God!
Than thine hath heaven itself a smile
More rich?   Are feet of angels shod
With peace more fair?   O month divine!
Stay, till thy tranquil soul be mine.

To-morrow.

One walks secure in wisdom-trodden ways
That lead to peaceful nights through happy days—
Health, fame, friends, children, and a gentle wife,
All Youth can covet or Experience praise,
And Use withal to crown the ease of life.
   Ah, thirsting for another day,
     How dread the fear
  If he but knew the danger near!

Robert Underwood Johnson.

Another, with some old inheritance
Of Fate, unmitigated yet by Chance, —
Condemned by those he loves, with no appeal
To his own fearful heart, that ever pants
For newer circlings of the cruel Wheel !
  Ah, thirsting for another day,
    What need of fear
  If he but knew the help that's near ?

———

Samuel Minturn Peck.

[Born at Tuskaloosa, Alabama, 1854. The poems selected are three of the author's own favorites and are quoted by his permission. "A Knot of Blue" from "Cap and Bells" (1886), and the other two pieces from "Rings and Love-Knots" (1893), Frederick A. Stokes Co., publishers.]

A Knot of Blue.

For the Boys of Yale.

She hath no gems of lustre bright
  To sparkle in her hair ;
No need hath she of borrowed light
  To make her beauty fair.
Upon her shining locks afloat
  Are daisies wet with dew,
And peeping from her lissome throat
  A little knot of blue.

A dainty knot of blue,
  A ribbon blithe of hue,
It fills my dreams with sunny gleams,—
  That little knot of blue.

125

I met her down the shadowed lane,
  Beneath the apple-tree,
The balmy blossoms fell like rain
  Upon my love and me ;
And what I said or what I did
  That morn I never knew
But to my breast there came and hid
  A little knot of blue.

A little knot of blue,
  A love knot strong and true,
'Twill hold my heart till life shall part,
  That little knot of blue.

Mignon.

Across the gloom the gray moth speeds
  To taste the midnight brew,
The drowsy lilies tell their beads
  On rosaries of dew.
    The stars seem kind,
    And e'en the wind
Hath pity for my woe,
Ah, must I sue in vain, *ma belle?*
    Say no, Mignon, say no !

Ere long the dawn will come to break
  The web of darkness through ;
Let not my heart unanswered ache
  That beats alone for you.
    Your casement ope
    And bid me hope,
Give me one smile to bless ;
A word will ease my pain, *ma belle*,
    Say yes, Mignon, say yes !

The Grapevine Swing.

When I was a boy on the old plantation
  Down by the deep bayou,
The fairest spot of all creation,
  Under the arching blue ;
When the wind came over the cotton and corn,
  To the long slim loop I'd spring
With brown feet bare, and a hat-brim torn,
  And swing in the grapevine swing.

Swinging in the grapevine swing,
Laughing where the wild birds sing,
  I dream and sigh
  For the days gone by,
Swinging in the grapevine swing.

Out—o'er the water-lilies bonnie and bright,
  Back—to the moss-grown trees;
I shouted and laughed with a heart as light
  As a wild-rose tossed by the breeze.
The mocking-bird joined in my reckless glee,
  I longed for no angel's wing,
I was just as near heaven as I wanted to be,
  Swinging in the grapevine swing.

Swinging in the grapevine swing,
Laughing where the wild birds sing,—
  Oh to be a boy
  With a heart full of joy,
Swinging in the grapevine swing!

I'm weary at noon, I'm weary at night,
  I'm fretted and sore of heart,
And care is sowing my locks with white
  As I wend through the fevered mart.
I'm tired of the world with its pride and pomp,
  And fame seems a worthless thing.
I'd barter it all for one day's romp,
  And a swing in the grapevine swing,

Swinging in the grapevine swing,
Laughing where the wild birds sing,
  I would I were away
  From the world to-day,
Swinging in the grapevine swing.

H. C. Bunner.

[Born 1855. 1896. The poems selected are reprinted by the author's permission.]

The Heart of the Tree.

AN ARBOR-DAY SONG.

What does he plant who plants a tree?
  He plants the friend of sun and sky;
He plants the flag of breezes free;
  The shaft of beauty, towering high;
  He plants a home to heaven anigh
    For song and mother-croon of bird
    In hushed and happy twilight heard—
The treble of heaven's harmony—
These things he plants who plants a tree.

What does he plant who plants a tree?
  He plants cool shade and tender rain,
And seed and bud of days to be,
  And years that fade and flush again;
  He plants the glory of the plain;
    He plants the forest's heritage;
    The harvest of a coming age;
The joy that unborn eyes shall see—
These things he plants who plants a tree.

J   129

What does he plant who plants a tree?
  He plants, in sap and leaf and wood,
In love of home and loyalty
  And far-cast thought of civic good—
His blessing on the neighborhood
    Who in the hollow of His hand
    Holds all the growth of all our land—
A nation's growth from sea to sea
Stirs in his heart who plants a tree.

An Old-Fashioned Love-Song.

Tell me what within her eyes
Makes the forgotten Spring arise,
And all the day, if kind she looks,
Flow to a tune like tinkling brooks ;
Tell me why, if but her voice
Falls on men's ears, their souls rejoice ;
Tell me why, if only she
Doth come into the companie
All spirits straight enkindled are,
As if a moon lit up a star.

Tell me this that's writ above,
And I will tell you why I love.

D. C. Sonnet.

Tell me why the foolish wind
Is to her tresses ever kind,
And only blows them in such wise
As lends her beauty some surprise ;
Tell me why no changing year
Can change from Spring if she appear;
Tell me why to see her face
Begets in all folk else a grace
That makes them fair, as love of her
Did to a gentler nature stir.

Tell me why, if she but go
Alone across the fields of snow,
All fancies of the Springs of old
Within a lover's breast grow bold ;
Tell me why, when her he sees,
Within him stirs an April breeze ;
And all that in his secret heart
Most sacredly was set apart,
And most was hidden, then awakes,
At the sweet joy her coming makes.

Tell me what is writ above,
And I will tell you why I love.

———— ————

Charles Henry Lüders.

[Born in Philadelphia, Penn., 1858. Died, 1891. The poem quoted is said to have been the author's favorite piece.]

The Four Winds.

Wind of the North,
Wind of the Norland snows,
Wind of the winnowed skies, and sharp, clear stars—
Blow cold and keen across the naked hills,
And crisp the lowland pools with crystal films,
And blur the casement squares with glittering ice,
But go not near my love.

Wind of the West,
Wind of the few, far clouds,
Wind of the gold and crimson sunset lands—
Blow fresh and pure across the peaks and plains,
And broaden the blue spaces of the heavens,
And sway the grasses and the mountain pines,
But let my dear one rest.

Wind of the East,
Wind of the sunrise seas,
Wind of the clinging mists and gray, harsh rains—
Blow moist and chill across the wastes of brine,
And shut the sun out, and the moon and stars,
And lash the boughs against the dripping eaves,
Yet keep thou from my love.
But thou, sweet wind !
Wind of the fragrant South,
Wind from the bowers of jasmine and of rose—
Over magnolia glooms and lilied lakes
And flowering forests come with dewy wings,
And stir the petals at her feet, and kiss
The low mound where she lies.

James Benjamin Kenyon.

[Born at Frankport, New York, 1858. The poems selected are quoted by permission of the author.]

A Sea Grave.

Yea, rock him gently in thine arms, O Deep!
  No nobler heart was ever hushed to rest
  Upon the chill, soft pillow of thy breast—
No truer eyes didst thou e'er kiss to sleep.
While o'er his couch the wrathful billows leap,
  And mighty winds roar from the darkened west,
  Still may his head on thy cool weeds be pressed,
Far down where thou dost endless silence keep.
Oh, when, slow moving through thy spaces dim
  Some scaly monster seeks its coral cave,
And pausing o'er the sleeper, stares with grim
  Dull eyes a moment downwards through the wave,
Then let thy pale green shadows curtain him,
  And swaying sea-flowers hide his lonely grave.

135

" My Love is Like the Vastness of the Sea."

My love is like the vastness of the sea,
   As deep as life, as high as heaven is high,
   And pure as an unclouded summer sky,
And as enduring as eternity.
My love is that which was, and is to be,
   Which knows no change, and which can never die;
   Which all the wealth of Ophir could not buy,
Yet free to *one* as light and air is free.
O Love, thou putt'st to shame the nightingale;
   Thy lips, like bees, are fraught with hydromel;
Than lilies are thy bosom is more pale;
   Thy words are sweeter than a silver bell:
      Yet time from thee thy beauties shall estrange:
      But this my Love can never suffer change.

Richard Eugene Burton.

[Born at Hartford, Conn., 1859. Graduated at Johns Hopkins University. The poem selected is reprinted by permission of the author.]

The City.

They do neither plight nor wed
In the city of the dead,
In the city where they sleep away the hours ;
But they lie, while o'er them range
Winter-blight and summer-change,
And a hundred happy whisperings of flowers.
No, they neither wed nor plight,
And the day is like the night,
For their vision is of other kind than ours.

They do neither sing nor sigh,
In that burgh of by and by
Where the streets have grasses growing cool and long ;
But they rest within their bed,
Leaving all their thoughts unsaid,
Deeming silence better far than sob or song.
No, they neither sigh nor sing,
Though the robin be a-wing,
Though the leaves of autumn march a million strong

There is only rest and peace
In the City of Surcease
From the failings and the wailings 'neath the Sun,
And the wings of the swift years
Beat but gently o'er the biers,
Making music to the sleepers every one.
There is only peace and rest ;
But to them it seemeth best,
For they lie at ease and know that life is done.

———————

Frank Dempster Sherman.

[Born at Peekskill, New York, 1860. The poems selected are quoted by permission of the author and by special arrangement with his publishers, Houghton, Mifflin & Co., Boston.]

Breath of Song.

From the minster's organ-loft,
  Floating down the shadowed nave,
Comes a stream of music soft,
  Falling as a weary wave
      Falls upon the beach of sand,
      Murmurous and sweet and bland,
      Bearing from the mighty sea
      Messages of melody.

There, alone, the organist
  Lets his listless fingers go—
Lost in a melodious mist—
  O'er the key-board, to and fro :
      There, half-dreaming in the gloom,
      Sits the weaver at his loom,
      Weaving with the threads of sound
      Music-woof the warp around.

All unconsciously he hides
  Strains familiar in his theme
When a master spirit glides
  Through the doorway of his dream :
      Mozart, Handel, Chopin, or
      Harmony's great conjuror—
      Rapt Beethoven !—each is part
      Of the dreaming player's heart.

So the poet dreams, nor heeds
  Who may listen, who may hear ;
Following where Fancy leads,
  She alone to him is dear :
      Omar, Keats, Theocritus,
      In his voice may speak to us
      From the realm of ages dim—
      These are in the heart of him !

Poets in the fields of Time,
  Since the world began, have sown
Wide the precious seeds of rhyme,
  And to us to-day are blown
      Odors from these poem-flowers—
      Seedlings of the later hours—
      Blossoming the fields along,
      Breathing the sweet breath of song.

The Library.

Give me the room whose every nook
Is dedicated to a book,
Two windows will suffice for air
And grant the light admission there ;
One looking to the south, and one
To speed the red, departing sun.
The eastern wall from friese to plinth
Shall be the Poet's labyrinth,
Where one may find the lords of rhyme
From Homer's down to Dobson's time ;
And at the northern side a space
Shall show an open chimney-place,
Set round with ancient tiles that tell
Some legend old and weave a spell
About the firedog-guarded seat,
Where one may dream and taste the heat :
Above, the mantel should not lack
For curios and bric-a-brac, —
Not much, but just enough to light
The room up when the fire is bright.
The volumes on this wall should be
All prose and all philosophy,

141

From Plato down to those who are
The dim reflections of that star ;
And these tomes all should serve to show
How much we write—how little know;
For since the problem first was set
No one has ever solved it yet.
Upon the shelves toward the west
The scientific books shall rest ;
Beside them, History; above,—
Religion, —hope, and faith, and love :
Lastly, the southern wall should hold
The story-tellers, new and old ;
Haroun al Raschid, who was truth
And happiness to all my youth,
Shall have the honored place of all
That dwell upon this sunny wall,
And with him there shall stand a throng
Of those who help mankind along
More by their fascinating lies
Than all the learning of the wise.

Such be the library; and take
This motto of a Latin make
To grace the door through which I pass:
Hic habitat Felicitas !

Attainment.

From the marble of his thought
Are the poet's fancies wrought
Into forms of symmetry,
Into rhyme and melody:
Not by any magic feat
Comes the statue forth complete ;
Only patient labor, long,
Can create the perfect song ;
Only love that does not tire
Can attain its high desire,—
Love that deems no gift of time
Wasted, so it win the rhyme
One elusive word to start
Life within the lyric's heart.
Still the Parthenon for us—
Jewel of Pentelicus
Fashioned centuries ago—
Shines with undiminished glow ;
Still the resurrected bust,
Buried ages in the dust,
Holds to-day its honored place
By the marvel of its grace ;

So the poet's song shall shine
For the jewel of one line ;
So his lyric shall endure
Be the carven marble pure.
Toil he must if he would win
Heaven's gate and enter in ;
Labor of a life-time give
That the sculptured verse shall live!

Clinton Scollard.

[Born at Clinton, New York, 1860. The poems quoted are reprinted by the author's permission.]

The Hunter.

Through dewy glades ere morn is high,
When fleecy cloud-ships sail the sky,
  With buoyant step and gun a-shoulder
And song on lip he wanders by.

He feels the cool air fan his brow,
He scents the spice of pine-tree bough,
  And lists, from moss-encrusted boulder,
The thrush repeat her matin vow.

Afar he hears the ringing horn,
And, from the rustling fields of corn,
  The harvest music welling over,
Greeting the autumn day, new-born.

In pendant purple globes he sees
The wild grapes hang amid the trees,
  And, from the last red buds of clover,
The darting flight of golden bees.

145

K

He marks the fiery crimson gleam
On wide primeval woods, that seem
   Like armored hosts with banners flying
That march when weary warriors dream.

Before him long-eared rabbits pass
Like shadows through the aisles of grass;
   From copses, wren to wren replying,
Utter for him a morning mass.

He does not heed the partridge's drum,
The squirrel's chattering, nor the hum
   Of myriad noises that, incessant,
Down dusky forest arches come.

He crosses quiet nooks of shade,
With flickering sunlight interlaid,
   Where, when outshines the silver crescent
Flit by the pixies, half afraid.

Thus on and on he blithely speeds,
Through briery brake and tangled reeds,
   Thinking of Robin and his bowmen
And all the archer's daring deeds;

Till 'neath a slope by vines o'ergrown,
Where, in the ages that have flown,
   The redmen slew their swarthy foemen,
He stands beside a pool alone.

Clinton Scollard.

Deep in the thicket, dense and dim,
That skirts the water's rushy rim,
  He crouches low and keenly listens
For sound of hoof or stir of limb.

At length he sees within the sheen
Of trembling leafage, darkly green,
  A lustrous eye that softly glistens,
And then a head of royal mien.

The startled hillsides sharply ring,
And answering echoes backward fling,
  While prone, upon the earth before him,
A proud red deer lies quivering.

He swings his prize to shoulders strong,
Then homeward swiftly strides along;
  The great blue skies a-smiling o'er him,
And all around the birds in song.

Behind the woods the sun creeps down,
And leaves thereon a crimson crown;
  From sapphire portals, pale and tender,
Venus o'erlooks the meadows brown.

And now that shadows hide the lane
Where rolled the orchard-laden wain,
  His weary feet upon the fender,
He slays the red deer o'er again !

147

The Snowdrop.

You ask why Spring's fair first-born flower is white :
  Peering from out the warm earth long ago,
  It saw above its head great drifts of snow,
And blanched with fright.

Pomona.

At noon of night the goddess, silver-stoled,
  Came with light foot across the moonlit land,
  And breezes soft as blow o'er Samarcand
Stirred her free hair that glinted like clear gold ;
Sweet were her smiling lips, as when of old
  Vertumnus wooed her on the grassy strand
  Of some swift Tuscan river overspanned
By sunny skies that knew no breath of cold.
So when the door of dawn grew aureate,
  And broken was the dim night's peaceful hush
  By harvesters uprisen to greet the morn,
They knew Pomona had passed by in state,
  For on the apples was a rosier blush,
  And on the grapes a richer lustre born.

Clinton Scollard.

The Statue.

As perfect in their symmetry as thine,
  O inarticulate marble lips, were those
  My love once raised to mine, yet tinged with rose
And freighted with a redolence divine.
Her poise of head was queenly ; fair and fine
  Her alabaster arms that shamed the snows ;
  Her gracious bearing had thy pure repose,
And stately was she as the forest pine.
Knowledge sat throned upon her regal brow,
  Round which her tresses rippled, bright as gold ;
Sweet as a songbird's on a budding bough
  The liquid voice that from her lips outrolled ;
But lo ! there came an awful change, and now
  Thou, in thine icy hush, art not more cold !

Richard Hovey.

[Born in Illinois, 1864. The poem quoted was selected by the author for this anthology.]

The Wander-Lovers.

Down the world with Marna !
That's the life for me !
Wandering with the wandering wind,
Vagabond and unconfined !
Roving with the roving rain
Its unboundaried domain !
Kith and kin of wander-kind,
Children of the sea !

Petrels of the sea-drift !
Swallows of the lea !
Arabs of the whole wide girth
Of the wind-encircled earth !
In all climes we pitch our tents,
Cronies of the elements,
With the secret lords of birth
Intimate and free.

151

All the seaboard knows us
From Fundy to the Keys ;
Every bend and every creek
Of abundant Chesapeake ;
Ardise hills and Newport coves
And the far-off orange groves,
Where Floridian oceans break,
Tropic tiger seas.

Down the world with Marna,
Tarrying there and here !
Just as much at home in Spain
As in Tangier or Touraine !
Shakespeare's Avon knows us well,
And the crags of Neufchâtel ;
And the ancient Nile is fain
Of our coming near.

Down the world with Marna,
Daughter of the air !
Marna of the subtle grace,
And the vision in her face !
Moving in the measures trod
By the angels before God !
With her sky-blue eyes amaze
And her sea-blue hair !

Richard Dovey.

Marna with the trees' life
In her veins a-stir !
Marna of the aspen heart
Where the sudden quivers start !
Quick-responsive, subtle, wild !
Artless as an artless child,
Spite of all her reach of art !
Oh, to roam with her !

Marna with the wind's will,
Daughter of the sea !
Marna of the quick disdain,
Starting at the dream of stain !
At a smile with love aglow,
At a frown a statued woe,
Standing pinnacled in pain
Till a kiss sets free !

Down the world with Marna,
Daughter of the fire !
Marna of the deathless hope,
Still alert to win new scope
Where the wings of life may spread
For a flight unhazarded !
Dreaming of the speech to cope
With the heart's desire !

153

Marna of the far quest
After the divine !
Striving ever for some goal
Past the blunder-god's control !
Dreaming of potential years
When no day shall dawn in fears !
That's the Marna of my soul,
Wander-bride of mine !

———

Madison J. Cawein.

[Born at Louisville, Kentucky, 1865. The poems quoted were selected by the author for this anthology.]

The Old Inn.

Red-winding from the sleepy town,
    One takes the lone, forgotten lane
Straight through the hills.   A brush-bird brown
    Bubbles in thorn-flowers sweet with rain ;
    Wind-shivers wave the wrinkled grain ;
The cautious drip of upper leaves
    Dips under leaves that drip again.—
Above the tangled tops it heaves
Its gables and its haunted eaves.

One creeper, gnarled to bloomlessness,
    O'er-forests all its eastern wall ;
The sighing cedars rake and press
    Dark boughs along the panes they sprawl :
    While, where the sun beats, comes the drawl
Of hiving wasps ; a bushy bee
    Gold-dusty, hurls along the hall
And hums into a crack.—To me
The shadows seem too scared to flee.

155

Of ragged chimneys martins make
　　Huge pipes of music ; twittering here
They build and roost.—My footfalls make
　　Strange stealing echoes, till I fear
　　I'll meet my pale self coming near,
My phantom face as in a glass ;
　　Or one men murdered, buried—where?—
Dim in gray, stealthy glimmer, pass
With lips that seem to moan "Alas."

From " Intimations of the Beautiful."

II.

The gods of Greece are mine once more !
　　The old philosophies again !
For I have drunk the hellebore
　　Of dreams, and dreams have made me sane—
The wine of dreams ! that doth unfold
　　My other self,—'mid shadowy shrines
Of myths which marble held of old,
Part of the Age of Bronze or Gold,—
　　That lives a pagan 'mid the pines.

Dead myths, to whom such dreams belong !
  O beautiful philosophies
Of Nature ! crystallised in song
  And marble, peopling lost seas,
Lost forests and the star-lost vast,
  Grant me the childlike faith that clung—
Through loveliness that could not last—
To Heaven in the pagan past,
  Calling for God with infant tongue !

LXVI.

The song-birds ? are they flown away ?
  The song-birds of the summer-time,
That sang their souls into the day,
  And set the laughing days to rhyme ?—
No catbird scatters through the hush
  The sparkling crystals of its song ;
Within the woods no hermit-thrush
  Trails an enchanted flute along,
A sweet assertion of the hush.

All day the crows fly cawing past ;
  The acorns drop ; the forests scowl :
At night I hear the bitter blast
  Hoot with the hooting of the owl.
The wild creeks freeze ; the ways are strewn
  With leaves that rot : beneath the tree
The bird that set its toil to tune,
  And made a home for melody,
Lies dead beneath the death-white moon.

Elizabeth Akers.

[Mrs. Akers Allen was born at Strong, Maine, 1832. Her first husband was Paul Akers, the famous sculptor. The poem quoted has been revised for this anthology by the author.]

The Sunset-Bird.

Is it a dream? The day is done,
  The long, warm, fragrant summer day;
Afar beyond the hills, the sun
  In purple splendor sinks away;
The fire-fly lights her floating spark,
  While here and there the first large stars
Look out, impatient for the dark;
  The cows stand waiting by the bars;
A group of children saunters by
  Toward home, with laugh and sportive word,
One pausing as she hears the high
  Soft prelude of an unseen bird—
    " *Sweet—sweet—sweet—*
      Sorrowful—sorrowful—sorrowful!"

159

Hist ! how that clear, aerial tone
  Makes all the hearkening woodland still !
Dear twilight voice that sings alone !
  And all the child's quick pulses thrill ;
Forgotten in her heedless hand
  The half-filled berry-basket swings ;
What cares she that the merry band
  Goes on and leaves her there ?   He sings !
Sings as a seraph shut from heaven
  And vainly seeking ingress there,
Might pour upon the listening even
  His love, and longing, and despair ;
    " Sweet—sweet—sweet—
      Sorrowful—sorrowful—sorrowful !"

Deep in the wood, whose giant pines
  Tower dark against the western sky,
While sunset's last faint crimson shines,
  He trills his marvellous ecstasy ;
With soul and sense entranced, she hears
  The wondrous pathos of his strain,
While from her eyes, unconscious tears
  Fall softly, born of tenderest pain.
What cares the rapt and dreaming child
  That duskier shadows gather round ?

Elizabeth Akers.

She only hears that flood of wild
  Melodious, melancholy sound—
    " *Sweet—sweet—sweet—*
      Sorrowful—sorrowful—sorrowful!"

O, wondrous spirit of the wood !
  No sky-lark, bearing up to heaven
His morning-hymn of gratitude,—
  No nightingale, that chants at even
Amid the red pomegranate blooms—
  No bulbul, in his fragrant dell
Where Persia's rose-fields breathe perfumes,
  Knows half the passionate tale you tell
To hearts which never can forget !
  O, lonely voice among the pines,
She hears its ringing music yet
  When sunset's last faint crimson shines—
    " *Sweet—sweet—sweet—*
      Sorrowful—sorrowful—sorrowful!"

Down from immeasurable heights
  The clear notes drop like crystal rain,
The echo of all lost delights,
  All youth's high hopes, all hidden pain,
All love's soft music, heard no more,
  But dreamed-of and remembered long-

L.

Ah, how can mortal bird outpour
  Such human heart-break in a song?
What can he know of lonely years,
  Of idols only raised to fall,
Of broken faith and secret tears?
  And yet his strain repeats them all—
    " *Sweet—sweet—sweet—*
      Sorrowful—sorrowful—sorrowful!"

Ah, still amid Maine's darkling pines,
  Lofty, mysterious, remote,
While sunset's last faint crimson shines,
  That singer's resonant echoes float ;
And she, the child of long ago,
  Who listened till the west grew gray,
Has learned, in later days, to know
  The mystic meaning of his lay ;
And often still in waking dreams
  Of youth's lost summer-times, she hears
Again that thrilling song, which seems
  The voice of dead and buried years—
    " *Sweet—sweet—sweet—*
      Sorrowful—sorrowful—sorrowful!"

ANNE REEVE ALDRICH.

Anne Reeve Aldrich.

[Born in New York City, 1866. Died in 1892. The poems quoted are selected from the posthumous volume, "Songs about Life, Love, and Death," and are reprinted with the permission of Charles Scribner's Sons, New York.]

A Crowned Poet.

In thy coach of state
    Pass, O King, along:
He no envy feels
    To whom God giveth song.

Starving, still I smile,
    Laugh at want and wrong:
He is fed and crowned
    To whom God giveth song.

Better than all pomps
    That to rank belong, —
One such dream as his
    To whom God giveth song.

Let us greet, O King,
    As we pass along:
He, too, is a king
    To whom God giveth song.

163

Insomnia.

O would God call a halt,—one moment's halt
  To that procession marching through my brain!
I would awake in thankful quiet, lie
  And watch the long defile begin again;
Would make no further dry-mouthed moans for sleep;
  Would take up patience in sweet hope's default,
And mutely bear the burthen of the hours,—
  If God would call a halt,—one moment's halt!

The Ring.

Hid in an antique box,
  With faded leaf and flower
(The only fitting gifts
  Of love that lives an hour),
Gemmed with a diamond tear
  For joy that could not cling,
Behold the word inside,
  For " *Toujours*," says the ring!

164

Anne Reeve Aldrich.

She sometimes lifts the lid,
  With light and careless laugh,
And reads the lying word,
  Love's mocking epitaph.
She has no sighs or tears
  For such a foolish thing
As love dead long ago,
  Yet—" *Toujours*," says the ring !

But in soft nights of May
  The proud and silent heart
Owns to itself a truth,
  And spurns its wonted part.
It cries out for the grace
  Of one departed spring,
" *Toujours*," admits the soul,
  And " *Toujours*," says the ring !

A Little Parable.

I made the cross myself whose weight
  Was later laid on me.
This thought is torture as I toil
  Up life's steep Calvary.

To think mine own hands drove the nails !
   I sang a merry song,
And chose the heaviest wood I had
   To build it firm and strong.

If I had guessed—if I had dreamed
   Its weight was meant for me,
I should have made a lighter cross
   To bear up Calvary.

————————

Charlotte Fiske Bates.

[Born in New York City, 1838. She assisted Longfellow in compiling his "Poems of Places." Died in 1889.]

Love's Rivals.

I.

Love, who devoutly lovest me,
I knew well when I wedded thee
    That, soon or late,
Death would come knocking at the gate,
Our happy breath to separate ;
    And thou or I
    Some by and by
Would hear throughout an empty heart
The awful echo—" Till Death part."
I knew how idly one must wait
Were either laid in stony state,
    Where lid nor lip is stirred,
The great Divorcer's voice once being heard.

II.

Ah, me! why did I never think
How often I must touch the brink
   Of such a woe?
For lovely Sleep I count a foe!
When in her arms thou liest low,
   Deaf, blind and dumb
   Dost thou become.
My eyes may beam on thee in vain
When thine have felt Sleep's lotus chain;
Unheeded I may come or go
Whenever she will have it so.
   True Love, I doubly weep,
Seeing I have two rivals, Death and Sleep.

Bessie Chandler.

[Bessie Chandler Parker was born in Batavia, N. Y., where she still lives. The poems selected are quoted with the author's permission.]

Brothers of Antaeus.

There was a giant, in the ages olden,
  Greater than other giants from his birth,
Who for his strength and courage was beholden
  To her, that mightiest of Mothers,—Earth.

And just to show him that she held him dearer
  Than other men, and watched and loved him more,
Each time, he touched her close,—came near and nearer,
  She made him stronger than he was before.

Though he were spent with wasting wounds unnumbered,
  Gained in fierce conflict with the sons of men,
He laid his head in her great lap and slumbered,
  And when he wakened he was strong again.

Antaeus, dost thou know our hearts are beating
  With the same blood that throbbed in thine at birth?
Across the centuries we send thee greeting,—
  We are thy brothers, born of that same earth.

Though through the year, we travel on as strangers
  That wander far from her who loves them best,
Meeting with many sorrows, many dangers,
  Looking in vain, for any place of rest,

See, how we thrill when Spring's white buds are bursting,
  See how we start when first the robins call,—
See how we rush, to our great Mother thirsting,
  Just for one look, of her who made us all !

We know her, in the pussy-willow's gleaming,
  We hear her in the nesting bird's low song,
Where drowsy ferns awaken from their gleaming,
  And wild flowers bloom, we touch her, and grow strong.

With gladdened eyes we look at one another,
  We have no fear of coming evil then,
For, like Antaeus, we have touched our Mother,
  And in that touch she makes us strong again !

How to Love.

Love me, but let me never know
  That I the limit of your love may touch ;
Always beyond my reach, below, above,
I want to feel that I may find your love.
    Love me, but—not too much.

Bessie Chandler.

Paint it in quiet, tender tints:
　　The fragrant flowers of spring wear such,
And summer lies beyond them.　In a blaze
Of brilliant hues the fall flowers end their days.
　　　　Love me, but—not too much.

Let it be like the soft blue sky,
　　That folds the earth around with gentle touch ;
Not like the crimson clouds at set of sun,
For darkness follows them, and day is done.
　　　　Love me, but—not too much.

Like the new moon I want your love :
　　My life will brighten 'neath its pure white touch.
The full moon gives great floods of silver light,
And then—it fades from out the starry night.
　　　　Love me, but—not too much.

But like the ivy, let love grow,
　　Slowly, unceasing, reaching wide and high,
Till it embraces all in its strong grasp,
And holds with true, unfading, living clasp.
　　　　So love me till I die !

Helen Gray Cone.

[Born in New York City, 1859. Teacher of English literature in New York Normal College. The poem selected is quoted by permission of the author, from her volume "The Ride to the Lady," and by special arrangement with her publishers, Houghton, Mifflin & Co., Boston.]

The Ride to the Lady.

"Now since mine even is come at last,—
  For I have been the sport of steel,
And hot life ebbeth from me fast,
  And I in saddle roll and reel, —
Come bind me, bind me on my steed !
Of fingering leech I have no need !"
The chaplain clasped his mailèd knee.
"Nor need I more thy whine and thee !
No time is left my sins to tell ;
But look ye bind me, bind me well !"
They bound him strong with leathern thong,
For the ride to the lady should be long.

Day was dying ; the poplars fled,
Thin as ghosts, on a sky blood-red ;
Out of the sky the fierce hue fell,
And made the streams as the streams of hell.

173

All his thoughts as a river flowed,
Flowed aflame as fleet he rode,
Onward flowed to her abode,
Ceased at her feet, mirrored her face.
(Viewless Death apace, apace,
Rode behind him in that race.)

"Face, mine own, mine alone,
Trembling lips my lips have known.
Birdlike stir of the dove-soft eyne
Under the kisses that make them mine!
Only of thee, of thee, my need!
Only to thee, to thee I speed!"
The Cross flashed by at the highway's turn;
In a beam of the moon the face shone stern.

Far behind had the fight's din died;
The shuddering stars in the welkin wide
Crowded, crowded, to see him ride.
The beating hearts of the stars aloof
Kept time to the beat of the horse's hoof.
"What is the throb that thrills so sweet?
Heart of my lady I feel it beat!"
But his own strong pulse the fainter fell,
Like the failing tongue of a hushing bell.
The flank of the great-limbed steed was wet
Not alone with the started sweat.

Helen Gray Gone.

Fast, and fast, and the thick black wood
Arched its cowl like a black friar's hood;
Fast, and fast, and they plunged therein,—
But the viewless rider rode to win.

Out of the wood to the highway's light
Galloped the great-limbed steed in fright;
The mail clashed cold, and the sad owl cried,
And the weight of the dead oppressed his side.

Fast, and fast, by the road he knew;
And slow, and slow, the stars withdrew;
And the waiting heaven turned weirdly blue,
As a garment worn of a wizard grim.
He neighed at the gate in the morning dim.

She heard no sound before her gate,
Though very quiet was her bower.
All was as her hand had left it late :
The needle slept on the broidered vine,
Where the hammer and spikes of the passion-flower
Her fashioning did wait.

On the couch lay something fair,
With steadfast lips and veilèd eyne ;
But the lady was not there.

On the wings of shrift and prayer,
Pure as winds that winnow snow,
Her soul had risen twelve hours ago.
The burdened steed at the barred gate stood,
No whit the nearer to his goal.
Now God's great grace assoil the soul
That went out in the wood !

Danske Dandridge.

[Born at Copenhagen, Denmark, 1858. Now lives at Shepherdstown, West Virginia. A frequent contributor to American periodicals. The poem selected is quoted by permission of the author.]

The Dead Moon.

I.

We are ghost-ridden :
  Through the deep night
Wanders a spirit,
  Noiseless and white.
Loiters not, lingers not, knoweth not rest ;
Ceaselessly haunting the East and the West.

She, whose undoing the ages have wrought,
Moves on to the time of God's rhythmical thought.
  In the dark, swinging sea,
    As she speedeth through space,
  She reads her pale image ;
    The wounds are agape on her face.
  She sees her grim nakedness
    Pierced by the eyes
  Of the spirits of God
    In their flight through the skies.

177

(Her wounds they are many and hollow.)
The Earth turns and wheels as she flies,
And this Spectre, this Ancient, must follow.

II.

When, in the æons,
   Had she beginning?
What is her story?
   What was her sinning?
Do the ranks of the Holy Ones
   Know of her crime?
Does it loom in the mists
   Of the birthplace of Time?
The stars, do they speak of her
   Under their breath,
"Will this Wraith be for ever
   Thus restless in death?"
On, through immensity,
   Sliding and stealing,
On through infinity,
   Nothing revealing.

III.

I see the fond lovers:
   They walk in her light:
They charge the "soft maiden"
   To bless their love-plight.

Danske Dandridge.

Does she laugh in her place,
As she glideth through space?
Does she laugh in her orbit with never a sound?
That to her, a dead body,
With nothing but rents in her round;
Blighted and marred;
Wrinkled and scarred;
Barren and cold;
Wizened and old;
That to her should be told,
That to her should be sung
The yearning and burning of them that are young?

IV.

Our Earth that is young,
That is throbbing with life,
Has fiery upheavals,
Has boisterous strife;
But she that is dead has no stir, breathes no air;
She is calm, she is voiceless, in lonely despair.

V.

We dart through the void:
We have cries, we have laughter:
The phantom that haunts us
Comes silently after.

This Ghost-lady follows,
   Though none hear her tread ;
On, on, we are flying,
   Still tracked by our Dead ;
By this white awful Mystery,
     Haggard, and dead.

———

Margaret Deland.

[Born in Alleghany, Penn., 1857. The two poems selected are quoted from "The Old Garden" by permission of the author, and by special arrangement with her publishers, Houghton, Mifflin & Co., Boston.]

June.

Upon the breast of smiling June
    Roses and lilies lie,
And round her yet is faint perfume
    Of violets, just gone by;

Green is her gown, with 'broidery
    Of blossoming meadow grass,
That ripples like a flowing sea
    When winds and shadows pass.

Her breast is belted by the blue
    Of succory, like the sky,
And purple heart's-ease clasp her too,
    And larkspur growing high;

Laced is her bodice green with vines,
    And dew the sun has kissed,
Jewels her scarf that faintly shines,
    In folds of morning mist!

The buttercups are fringes fair
   Around her small white feet,
And on the radiance of her hair
   Fall cherry-blossoms sweet ;

The dark laburnum's chains of gold
   She twists about her throat :
Perched on her shoulder, blithe and bold,
   The brown thrush sounds his note !

And blue of the far dappled sky
   That shows at warm, still noon,
Shines in her softly smiling eye—
   Oh ! who's so sweet as June ?

Affaire D'Amour.

One pale November day,
   Flying Summer paused,
      They say ·
And growing bolder,
O'er rosy shoulder
   Threw to her Lover such a glance,
   That Autumn's heart began to dance.
     (O happy Lover !)

Margaret Deland.

A leafless Peach-tree bold
  Thought for him she smiled,
     I'm told ;
  And, stirred by love,
  His sleeping sap did move,
Decking each naked branch with green
To show her that her look was seen !
    (Alas ! poor Lover !)

But Summer, laughing, fled,
  Nor knew he loved her !
     'Tis said
  The Peach-tree sighed,
  And soon he gladly died :
And Autumn, weary of the chase,
Came on at Winter's sober pace.
    (O careless Lover !)

Emily Dickinson.

[Born in Amherst, Mass., 1830. Died there in 1886. Her poems were not published till after her death. The pieces selected are quoted from "Poems," first and second series, published by Roberts Brothers, Boston.]

Success.

Success is counted sweetest
By those who ne'er succeed.
To comprehend a nectar
Requires sorest need.

Not one of all the purple host
Who took the flag to-day
Can tell the definition,
So clear, of victory,

As he, defeated, dying,
On whose forbidden ear
The distant strains of triumph
Break, agonized and clear.

Compensation.

For each ecstatic instant
We must an anguish pay
In keen and quivering ratio
To the ecstasy.

For each beloved hour
Sharp pittances of years,
Bitter contested farthings
And coffers heaped with tears.

———————

LOUISE IMOGEN GUINEY.

Louise Imogen Guiney.

[Born at Boston, Mass., 1861. The poems selected are quoted by permission of the author, and by special arrangement with her publishers, Houghton, Mifflin & Co., Boston.]

The Wild Ride.

I hear in my heart, I hear in its ominous pulses,

All day, the commotion of sinewy mane-tossing horses;

All night, from their cells, the importunate tramping and neighing.

Cowards and laggards fall back ; but alert to the saddle,

Straight, grim, and abreast, vault our weather-worn, galloping legion,

With a stirrup-cup each to the one gracious woman that loves him.

The road is thro' dolor and dread, over crags and morasses ;

There are shapes by the way, there are things that appal or entice us :

What odds? We are Knights, and our souls are but bent on the riding !

I hear in my heart, I hear in its ominous pulses,
All day, the commotion of sinewy, mane-tossing horses;
All night, from their cells, the importunate tramping and
  neighing.

We spur to a land of no name, out-racing the storm-wind ;
We leap to the infinite dark, like the sparks from the anvil.
Thou leadest, O God !   All's well with Thy troopers that
  follow.

The Light of the House.

Beyond the cheat of Time, here where you died you live ;
You pace the garden-walls secure and sensitive ;
You linger on the stair :   Love's lonely pulses leap !
The harpsichord is shaken, the dogs look up from sleep.

Years after, and years after, you keep your heirdom still,
Your winning youth about you, your joyous face and skill,
Unvexed, unapprehended, with waking sense adored ;
And still the house is happy that hath so dear a lord.

To every quiet inmate, strong in the cheer you brought,
Your name is as a spell midway of speech and thought ;
And unto whoso knocks, an awe-struck visitor,
The sunshine that was you floods all the open door !

Snow Falls.

Snow crowds into the day,
So woven, ray in ray,
  So vertical and wide,
It seems mere tremor of the air
  As heat at Lammastide.

Water is hid and bound.
The hilltops lower around,
  Away all noises creep.
On the shut eyelids of the wind
  Sinks more and more of sleep.

How large the old nests be
High on their frozen tree,
  Once little and warm and new !
Now is the time when reveries
  Turn cold and spacious too.

The buried houses look
Like some baptismal book
  Open to coming men;
In veils that spread from cloud to cloud
  Creation breeds again.

Who walks this minster white,
Down the grand reach of light
  Where flesh and faith dispart,
Sings. Even in courts and aisles of death,
  Death is not, and thou art !

——— ——— ———

GERTRUDE HALL

Gertrude Hall.

[Born in Boston, Mass. Educated in Italy. Her first volume, "Verses," appeared in 1890 and attracted wide attention. From that volume the poems selected are quoted by permission of the author.]

Night after Night.

Yes, I have wrestled with my giant, I:
   Night after night we twain renew our strife,
   And he, so strong I cannot get his life,
And I, weak, yet he cannot make me die.

He wrings my sinews with a grim delight,
   He grinds my heart as in an iron screw,
   Yet I defy—and he cannot subdue,
And so we twain wage war, night after night.

Night after night, until my life have end,
   I and my giant must stand face to face,
   He will not spare, and I shall not ask grace,
Ground, wrung, and broken—no! I will not bend.

At length, straight-gazing in his baleful eye,
   I shall say to my giant, "Thou wast strong,
   I, weak. My foe, have we not travailed long'
And still I am *not* vanquished—though I die."

191

" Be Good to Me."

Be good to me! If all the world united
  Should bend its powers to gird my youth with pain,
Still might I fly to thee—Dear—and be righted,—
  But if thou wrongst me—where shall I complain?

I am the dove a random shot surprises,
  That from her flight she droppeth quivering
And in the deadly arrow recognizes
  A blood-wet feather—once in her own wing.

" Thou by the River Musing."

Thou by the river musing,
  Maid of few summer-tides,
With dreamy eyes perusing
  Thy looking-glass that glides:

Somewhere the ship is booming
  Whose hold thy treasure hides,
Somewhere the castle looming
  Where thy true love abides.

Somewhere the wreath is blowing
  To crown thy hair a bride's—
Somewhere the stout oak growing
  To make thy coffin sides.

Ellen Mackay Hutchinson.

-[The poems selected are quoted from "Songs and Lyrics" (1881) by special arrangement with Houghton, Mifflin & Co., Boston.]

The Runaway.

Joy, my tender fairy,
Wilful, wistful, airy—
I pray you, tell me why
You are so very shy.

Don't I want you, love you,
Look and long to prove you
Friend, as I to you,
Faithful, gentle, true?

" You don't know how to find me;
You don't know how to bind me;
I fly, yet am not shy—
Shall I tell you why?

" Because, while you pursue,
My sweetness I renew;
I fold my wings to rest
In some less eager breast'"

The Quest.

It was a heavenly time of life
  When first I went to Spain,
The lovely land of silver mists,
  The land of golden grain.

My little ship through unknown seas
  Sailed many a changing day ;
Sometimes the chilling winds came up
  And blew across her way.

Sometimes the rain came down and hid
  The shining shores of Spain,
The beauty of the silver mists
  And of the golden grain.

But through the rains and through the winds,
  Upon the untried sea,
My fairy ship sailed on and on,
  With all my dreams and me.

And now, no more a child, I long
  For that sweet time again,
When on the far horizon bar
  Rose up the shores of Spain.

O lovely land of silver mists,
  O land of golden grain,
I look for you with smiles, with tears,
  But look for you in vain '

A Cry from the Shore.

Come down, ye graybeard mariners,
  Unto the wasting shore !
The morning winds are up,—the gods
  Bid me to dream no more.
Come, tell me whither I must sail,
  What peril there may be,
Before I take my life in hand
  And venture out to sea !

"We may not tell thee where to sail,
  Nor what the dangers are ;
Each sailor soundeth for himself,
  Each hath a separate star :
Each sailor soundeth for himself,
  And on' the awful sea
What we have learned is ours alone ;
  We may not tell it thee."

195

Come back, O ghostly mariners,
　　Ye who have gone before !
I dread the dark, impetuous tides ;
　　I dread the farther shore.
Tell me the secret of the waves ;
　　Say what my fate shall be—
Quick ! for the mighty winds are up,
　　And will not wait for me.

" Hail and farewell, O voyager !
　　Thyself must read the waves ;
What we have learned of sun and storm
　　Lies with us in our graves :
What we have learned of sun and storm
　　Is ours alone to know.
The winds are blowing out to sea,
　　Take up thy life and go ! "

———————

.

Helen Hunt Jackson.

[H. H.]

[Born at Amherst, Mass., 1831. She married, first, Captain Hunt, 1852; second, Wm. Jackson, 1875. Died in California, 1885. The poems are quoted from the collective edition of her poems, Roberts Brothers, Boston.]

Vanity of Vanities.

Bee to the blossom, moth to the flame ;
Each to his passion ; what's in a name ?

Red clover's sweetest, well the bee knows ;
No bee can suck it ; lonely it blows.

Deep lies its honey, out of reach, deep ;
What use in honey hidden to keep ?

Robbed in the autumn, starving for bread ;
Who stops to pity a honey-bee dead ?

Star-flames are brightest, blazing the skies;
Only a hand's breadth the moth-wing flies.

Fooled with a candle, scorched with a breath ;
Poor little miller, a tawdry death !

197

Life is a honey, life is a flame ;
Each to his passion ; what's in a name ?

Swinging and circling, face to the sun
Brief little planet, how it doth run !

Bee-time and moth-time, add the amount ;
White heat and honey, who keeps the count ?

Gone some fine evening, a spark out-lost !
The world no darker for one star lost !

Bee to the blossom, moth to the flame ;
Each to his passion ; what's in a name !

The Fir-Tree and the Brook.

The Fir-Tree looked on stars, but loved the Brook !
"O silver-voiced ! if thou wouldst wait,
My love can bravely woo."   All smiles forsook
The Brook's white face.   " Too late !
Too late !   I go to wed the sea.
I know not if my love would curse or bless thee.
I may not, dare not, tarry to caress thee.
    Oh, do not follow me !"

Helen Hunt Jackson.

The Fir-Tree moaned and moaned till spring ;
Then laughed in maniac joy to feel
Early one day, the woodmen of the King
Sign him with sign of burning steel,
The first to fall.   " Now flee
Thy swiftest, Brook !   Thy love may curse or bless me,
I care not, if but once thou dost caress me,
    O Brook, I follow thee !"

All torn and bruised with mark of axe and chain,
Hurled down the dizzy slide of sand,
Tossed by great waves in ecstasy of pain,
And rudely thrown at last to land,
The Fir-Tree heard :   " Oh, see
With what fierce love it is I must caress thee !
I warned thee I might curse, and never bless thee,
    Why did'st thou follow me ?"

All stately set with spar and brace and rope,
The Fir-Tree stood and sailed, and sailed.
In wildest storm when all the ship lost hope,
The Fir-Tree never shook nor quailed,
Nor ceased from saying, " Free
Art thou, O Brook !   But once thou hast caressed me ;
For life, for death, thy love has cursed or blessed me .
Behold, I follow thee !"

Lost in a night, and no man left to tell,
Crushed in the giant iceberg's play,
The ship went down without a song, a knell.
Still drifts the Fir-Tree night and day ;
Still moans along the sea
A voice : "O Fir-Tree I thus must I possess thee ;
Eternally, brave love, will I caress thee,
  Dead for the love of me !"

Fealty.

The thing I count and hold as fealty—
  The only fealty to give or take—
  Doth never reckoning keep, and coldly make
Bond to itself with this or that to be
Content as wage ; the wage unpaid, to free
  Its hand from service, and its love forsake,
  Its faith cast off, as one from dreams might wake
At morn, and smiling watch the vision flee.
Such fealty is treason in disguise,
  Who trusts it, his death-warrant sealed doth bear.
Love looks at it with angry, wondering eyes ;
  Love knows the face true fealty doth wear,
  The pulse that beats unchanged by alien air,
Or hurts, or crimes, until the loved one dies.

Emma Lazarus.

[Born in New York City, 1849. Died there in 1887. The poems selected are quoted by special permission of Houghton, Mifflin & Co., Boston.]

Success.

Oft have I brooded on defeat and pain,
　　The pathos of the stupid stumbling throng.
　　These I ignore to-day and only long
To pour my soul forth in one trumpet strain,
　　One clear, grief-shattering, triumphant song,
For all the victories of man's high endeavor,
Palm-bearing laurelled deeds that live forever,
　　The splendor clothing him whose will is strong.
Hast thou beheld the deep, glad eyes of one
　　Who has persisted and achieved? Rejoice!
On naught diviner shines the all-seeing sun.
　　Salute him with free heart and choral voice,
'Midst flippant, feeble crowds of spectres wan,
The bold, significant, successful man.

Among the Thousand Islands.

The misty air like amber seems,
  Like melting gold the sky o'erhead.
Athwart the ivory gate of dreams,
  Surely our bark is piloted.

For this is the enchanted realm,
  The fairy-palace reared by sleep ;
Through emerald chambers glides our helm,
  And in our wake flame-opals leap.

I need but lift my heavy eyes
  To South or North, to East or West,
To see, as at my bidding, rise
  A wave-charmed island's tufted crest.

Here a tall headland draped with fern,
  Pine-crowned and honey-combed with caves ;
There, just above the river's urn,
  A low, soft nest of grasses waves.

Now narrowing cliffs inclose our prow,
  Fantastic rocks streaked blue and rose ;
The channel eddies swift,—and now
  Broad as a sea the river flows.

Emma Lazarus.

Thrilled by the water's long embrace,
  The slender silver reeds are stirred,
And sway with slow, voluptuous grace,
  Like dancers to a waltz unheard.

There where the crystal floor scarce shines,
  So thick the velvet leaves unfold,
Superb the lily-queen reclines,
  A miracle of snow and gold.

Here is Miranda's island—look !
  'Twixt tree and cloud still Ariel flies,
Behind the hill, beyond the brook,
  The whelp of Sycorax yet lies.

But duke and princess, clown and seer,
  Have voyaged forth to other seas,
And fathom deep, since many a year,
  Are buried book and wand and keys.

No ribboned grass is floating there,
  Along our smooth, pearl-paven path,
But hidden faces' pale green hair
  Of nymphs and nereids at the bath.

On ! we shall find in sober sooth
   From some clear well-head bubbling up,
The fountain of eternal youth
   To brim the thirsty pilgrim's cup.

Enchanted world ! enchanted hour !
   Hail and farewell, enchanted stream,
That hast the unimagined power,
   To make the real surpass the dream !

Julie Mathilde Lippmann.

[Born in Brooklyn, N.Y., 1864. The poems are quoted by special permission of the author.]

The Leaf.

A mere leaf, I, 'mid manifold mere leaves :
   Worth naught unless to serve Spring at the start,
When she has need of greenness, and receives
   The littlest blade with hospitable heart.
Since even slight things win a welcome where
   The rule is no thing and the world is bare.

Mayhap it should content me that I wrought
   My tiny miracle of wonderment
Thro' lack of wonders—since I have not caught
   The trick of beauty nor the knack of scent.
Perchance it should suffice me that, in brief,
   'Mid manifold green leaves I am a leaf.

And so it would, had not (in that dear hour
   When God was planning roses, and had dream
Of framing pure perfection in a flower
   To pierce men's hearts with rapture, it would seem)
Some mystic hint of the supremely fair
   Found me, naught but a lowly leafling there.

So I have dreams of beauty that are pain,
  And still must dream them on, or else must die—
I would do more than tremble to the rain,
  Or flutter to the breeze that brushes by.
I am aware of joys which is the chief—
  But to what good, since I am but a leaf?

The rose and I were born of one stanch root ;
  We twain upon one stem live day by day :
She, of her royal rose-rights in pursuit,
  I, for what meagre ministries I may.
      .   .   .   .

O Nature, if renascent, I were fain
  Thou make me dreamless—or no leaf again !

A Song of the Road.

Come, comrades ! since the road is long
Let's liven it by tune and song,
And greeting give to all we pass :—
To white-of-head ; to light-of-head ;
To matron grave, and laughing lass :
　　Hurrah ! for lane and by-way ;
　　　　For distant path and nigh-way ;
　　　　For friends we greet, for foes we meet
　　Along the world's broad highway.

'Tis morning-break, lithe limbs are strong.
Who dreams of crime and guilt and wrong ?
Yon youngling and his violet-eyes ?
Nay ! light-of-mind and love-so-blind
Are wisdom-proof and folly-wise.
　　Hurrah ! for lane and by-way ;
　　　　For distant path and nigh-way ;
　　　　For friends we greet, for foes we meet
　　Along the world's broad highway.

'Tis noontide, let us spend an hour
Dream-drinking, ere we lose the power,
And all our pleasure disappears,
Since slight-of-heart and blight-of-heart
Have sworn the goblet smacks of tears.

Hurrah ! for lane and by-way;
  For distant path and nigh-way;
  For friends we greet, for foes we meet
Along the world's broad highway.

'Tis night, and lo ! foul thieves have mobbed
The weak ones here, and left them robbed
Of hope and faith and love and rest—
But sure-of-soul and pure-of-soul
Still fold their treasures to their breast :
  Hurrah ! for lane and by-way;
  For distant path and nigh-way;
  For every one whose journey's done—
Who's gained the distant skyway.

———————

HARRIET MONROE.

Harriet Monroe.

[Born in 1860. Author of "Valeria and other Poems" (1892).
Miss Monroe wrote the text of the cantata sung at the dedication of
the Chicago Auditorium in Dec., 1889. She also, by request of the
Committee of Ceremonies, wrote the Commemoration Ode read and
sung at the dedicatory ceremonies of the World's Columbian Exposi-
tion, on the 400th anniversary of the discovery of America.]

Origin of the Tides.

The moon, a lady robed in white,
  Rose o'er the bosom of the sea
And whispered: Take me ! by thy might
  Embrace me, seize me, set me free
From endless bondage to the night !

The brave sea rose to do her will,
  And tossed his pale arms high in air.
The deeps responded with a thrill
  That shook far coasts and islands fair.
Yet the pale maid rose higher still.

The bold surge, wrestling with defeat,
  Threw foamy kisses high—in vain.
At last he sighed: Ah, lady sweet,
  Thou art too great !   But thou shalt reign
My queen.   My heart shall rise to greet
The daily dancing of thy feet.

O

Song of the Air.

Hush—hush!   Ah, whisper low!
  Dost thou not know
    Asleep earth lies?
Nay—wake her not!   She hears
  The circling spheres
    Sing in their skies.

I love her.   All the day
  I ward away
    The sun's fierce scorn.
All night I sob and sing,
  And cool winds bring
    To soothe the morn.

I wrap her round with blue
  Her lord looks through
    With face of fire—
With blue so soft and pure
  She can endure
    His passion dire.

And when her spirit sighs
  White clouds arise
    To soothe the glare.
When she is sad, soft rains
  Efface her stains
    And leave her fair.

And though her beauty fall
  Beneath a pall
    As gray as death,
Though by fierce tempests torn
  She lies forlorn,
    Weary of breath—

I come with footfall soft
  And lift aloft
    Her robes of woe;
And from her lover down
  I bear a crown—
    The shining bow.

Then doth she ope her eyes
  In glad surprise,
    And smile to see
The sun's winged troops awake
  For her sweet sake,
    Her slaves to be.

And I, I lie as still
  As nights that thrill
    With dawns unborn;
I waft away her tears
  And soothe her fears—
    Sweet wraith forlorn.

So hush! She floats to-night
  On star streams bright;
    Her woes are gone.
The sweet moon sings to her.
  No leaf shall stir
    Until the dawn.

———

Harriet Monroe.

The Fortunate One.

Beside her ashen hearth she sate her down,
  Whence he she loved had fled ;
His children plucking at her sombre gown,
  And calling for the dead.

One came to her clad in the robes of May,
  And said sweet words of cheer,
Bidding her bear her burden in God's way,
  And feel her loved one near.

And she who spake thus would have given, thrice blest,
  Long lives of happy years,
To clasp his children to a mother's breast,
  And weep his widow's tears.

———————

Louise Chandler Moulton.

[Born at Pomfret, Conn., 1835.   Poet and novelist.   The poems selected are quoted with the permission of the author.]

A Painted Fan.

Roses and butterflies snared on a fan,
  All that is left of a summer gone by ;
Oh swift bright wings that flashed in the sun,
  And loveliest blossoms that bloomed to die ;

By what subtle spell did you lure them here—
  Fixing a beauty that will not change—
Roses whose petals never will fall,
  Bright, swift wings that never will range ?

Had you owned but the skill to snare as well
  The swift-winged hours that came and went,
To prison the words that in music died,
  And fix with a spell the heart's content,

Then had you been of magicians the chief ;
  And loved and lovers should bless your art,
If you could but have painted the soul of the thing,-
  Not the rose alone, but the rose's heart !

215

Flown are those days with their winged delights,
　As the odor is gone from the summer rose ;
Yet still, whenever I wave my fan,
　The soft, south wind of memory blows.

We Lay us Down to Sleep.

We lay us down to sleep,
　And leave to God the rest ;
Whether to wake and weep
　Or wake no more be best.

Why vex our souls with care ?
　The grave is cool and low ;
Have we found life so fair
　That we should dread to go ?

We've kissed love's sweet red lips,
　And left them sweet and red ;
The rose the wild bee sips
　Blooms on when he is dead.

Some faithful friends we've found,
　But they who love us best,
When we are under ground
　Will laugh on with the rest.

No task have we begun
  But other hands can take ;
No work beneath the sun
  For which we need to wake.

Then hold us fast, sweet Death,
  If so, it seemeth best
To Him who gave us breath
  That we should go to rest.

We lay us down to sleep,
  Our weary eyes we close ;
Whether to wake and weep
  Or wake no more, He knows.

" If There Were Dreams to Sell."

If there were dreams to sell,
Do I not know full well
  What I would buy ?
Hope's dear, delusive spell,
Its happy tale to tell—
  Joy's fleeting sigh.

I would be young again—
Youth's madding bliss and bane
        I would recapture—
Though it were keen with pain,
All else seems void and vain
        To that fine rapture.

I would be glad once more—
Slip through an open door
    .   Into Life's glory—
Keep what I spent of yore,
Find what I lost before—
        Hear an old story.

As it of old befell,
Breaking Death's frozen spell,
        Love should draw nigh :—
If there were dreams to sell
Do I not know too well
        What I would buy?

————

A Cry.

O wanderer in unknown lands, what cheer?
　How dost thou fare on thy mysterious way?
　What strange light breaks upon thy distant day,
Yet leaves me lonely in the darkness here?
O bide no longer in that far-off sphere,
　Though all Heaven's cohorts should thy footsteps stay.
　Break through their splendid, militant array,
And answer to my call, O dead and dear!

I shall not fear thee, howsoe'er thou come.
　Thy coldness will not chill, though Death *is* cold—
　A touch and I shall know thee, or a breath;
Speak the old, well-known language, or be dumb;
　Only come back! Be near me as of old,
　So thou and I shall triumph over Death!

Nora Perry.

[Born in Massachusetts, 1845. The poems selected are quoted by permission of the author, and by special arrangement with her publishers, Houghton, Mifflin & Co., Boston.]

Unattained.

Tired, tired and spent, the day is almost run,
    And oh, so little done !
Above, and far beyond, far out of sight,
    Height over height,
I know the distant hills I should have trod,—
    The hills of God,—
Lift up their airy peaks, crest over crest,
    Where I had prest
My faltering, weary feet, had strength been given,
    And found my way to Heaven.
Yet once, ah, once, the place where now I stand,
    The promised land
Seemed to my young, rapt vision, from afar.
    The morning star
Shone for my guidance, beckoned me along,
    As fresh and strong,
And all untried, untired I took my way
    At break of day.

The path looked strewn with flowers, in that white light,
    Each distant height
Smiled at me like a friend,—a faithful friend,—
    Sure that the end
Would soon, ah, soon, repay with sweet redress
    All weariness.
But when the time wore on, and in the bright
    And searching light
Of high noon-day, I lifted up my eyes,
    The purple dyes
Through which I had descried my mountain height,
    Had vanished quite.
Then, suddenly, I knew that I did stand
    Within the promised land
Of youth's fair dreams and hopes ; but with a thrill,
    I saw that still
Above, and far beyond, far out of sight,
    Height over height,
Lifted the fairer hills I should have trod,—
    The hills of God !

Riding Down.

O, did you see him riding down,
And riding down, while all the town
Came out to see, came out to see,
And all the bells rang mad with glee?

Oh, did you hear those bells ring out,
The bells ring out, the people shout,
And did you hear that cheer on cheer
That over all the bells rang clear?

And did you see the waving flags,
The fluttering flags, the tattered flags,
Red, white, and blue, shot through and through,
Baptized with battle's deadly dew?

And did you hear the drum's gay beat,
The drum's gay beat, the bugles sweet,
The cymbals clash, the cannon's crash,
That rent the sky with sound and flash?

And did you see me waiting there,
Just waiting there and watching there,
One little lass, amid the mass
That pressed to see the hero pass?

223

And did you see him smiling down,
And smiling down, as riding down
With slowest pace, with stately grace,
He caught the vision of a face,—

My face uplifted, red and white,
Turned red and white with sheer delight,
To meet the eyes, the smiling eyes,
Out flashing in their swift surprise?

O, did you see how swift it came,
How swift it came, like sudden flame,
That smile to me, to only me,
The little lass who blushed to see?

And at the windows all along,
O all along, a lovely throng
Of faces fair beyond compare,
Beamed out upon him riding there!

Each face was like a radiant gem,
A sparkling gem, and yet for them
No swift smile came, like sudden flame,
No arrowy glance took certain aim.

He turned away from all their grace,
From all that grace of perfect face,
He turned to me, to only me,
The little lass, who blushed to see!

Cressid.

Has any one seen my Fair,
Has any one seen my Dear?
Could any one tell me where
And whither she went from here?

The road is winding and long,
With many a turn and twist,
And one could easy go wrong,
Or ever one thought or list.

How should one know my Fair,
And how should one know my Dear?
By the dazzle of sunlight hair
That smites like a golden spear.

By the eyes that say " Beware,"
By the smile that beckons you near,—
This is to know my Fair,
This is to know my Dear.

Rough and bitter as gall
The Voice that suddenly comes
Over the windy wall
Where the fishermen have their homes:—

225

P

"Ay, ay, we know full well
The way your fair one went:
She led by the way of Hell,
And into its torments sent

"The boldest and bravest here,
Who knew nor guilt nor guile,
Who knew not shadow of fear
Till he followed that beckoning smile.

"Now would you find your Fair,
Now would you find your Dear?
Go, turn and follow her where
And whither she went from here,

"Along by the winding path
That leads by the old sea-wall:
The wind blows wild with wrath,
And one could easily fall

"From over the rampart there,
If one should lean too near,
To look for the sunlight hair
That smites like a golden spear!"

—

Tying Her Bonnet Under Her Chin.

Tying her bonnet under her chin,
She tied her raven ringlets in;
But not alone in the silken snare
Did she catch her lovely floating hair,
For, tying her bonnet under her chin,
She tied a young man's heart within.

They were strolling together up the hill,
Where the wind comes blowing merry and chill,
And it blew the curls a frolicsome race,
All over the happy peach-colored face,
Till, scolding and laughing, she tied them in,
Under her beautiful dimpled chin.

And it blew a color, bright as the bloom
Of the pinkest fuchsia's tossing plume,
All over the cheeks of the prettiest girl
That ever imprisoned a romping curl,
Or, tying her bonnet under her chin,
Tied a young man's heart within.

Steeper and steeper grew the hill;
Madder, merrier, chillier still
The western wind blew down, and played
The wildest tricks with the little maid
As, tying her bonnet under her chin,
She tied a young man's heart within.

O western wind, do you think it was fair,
To play such tricks with her floating hair?
To gladly, gleefully do your best
To blow her against the young man's breast,
Where he as gladly folded her in,
And kissed her mouth and her dimpled chin?

Ah Ellery Vane, you little thought,
An hour ago, when you besought
This country lass to walk with you,
After the sun had dried the dew,
What perilous danger you'd be in,
As she tied her bonnet under her chin!

Sarah Morgan Bryan Piatt.

[Born in Lexington, Kentucky, 1836. Wife of John James Piatt. The poems selected are quoted by permission of the author, and by special arrangement with her publishers, Houghton, Mifflin & Co., Boston.]

Last Words

OVER A LITTLE BED AT NIGHT.

Good night, pretty sleepers of mine—
    I never shall see you again :
Ah, never in shadow nor shine ;
    Ah, never in dew nor in rain !

In your small dreaming dresses of white,
    With the wild-bloom you gathered to-day,
In your quiet shut hands, from the light
    And the dark you will wander away.

Though no graves in the tree-haunted grass,
    And no love in the beautiful sky
Shall take you as yet, you will pass,
    With this kiss through these tear drops. Good by!

229

With less gold and more gloom in their hair,
   When the buds near have faded to flowers,
Three faces may wake here as fair—
   But older than yours are, by hours !

Good-night, then, lost darlings of mine,
   I never shall see you again :
Ah, never in shadow nor shine ;
   Ah, never in dew nor in rain !

Broken Promise.

After strange stars, inscrutable, on high ;
   After strange seas beneath his flowing feet ;
After the glare in many a brooding eye,—
   I wonder if the cry of " Land " was sweet ?

Or did the Atlantic gold, the Atlantic palm,
   The Atlantic bird and flower, seem poor, at best,
To the grey Admiral under sun and calm,
   After the passionate doubt and faith of quest ?

Spring-Song.

Blush and blow, blush and blow,
  Wind and brier-rose, if you will.
You are sweet enough, I know,—
You are sweet enough, but oh,
Hidden lonely, hidden low,
  There is something sweeter still.

Come and go, come and go,
  Suns of morning, moons of night.
You are fair enough, I know,—
You are fair enough, but oh,
Hidden darkly, hidden low
  Lies the light that gave you light.

Edna Dean Proctor.

[Born at Henniker, New Hampshire. The poems selected are quoted by permission of the author and by special arrangement with her publishers, Houghton, Mifflin & Co., Boston.]

The Brooklyn Bridge.

A granite cliff on either shore ;
    A highway poised in air ;
Above, the wheels of traffic roar ;
    Below, the fleets sail fair ;—
And in and out, forevermore,
The surging tides of ocean pour,
And past the towers the white gulls soar,
    And winds the sea-clouds bear.

O peerless this majestic street,
    This road that leaps the brine !
Upon its height twin cities meet,
    And throng its grand incline,--
To east, to west, with swiftest feet,
Though ice may crash and billows beat,
Though blinding fogs the wave may greet,
    Or golden summer shine.

Sail up the Bay with morning's beam,
        Or rocky Hellgate by,—
Its columns rise, its cables gleam,
        Great tents athwart the sky!
And lone it looms, august, supreme,
When, with the splendor of a dream,
Its blazing cressets gild the stream
        Till evening shadows fly.

By Nile stand proud the pyramids,
        But they were for the dead ;
The awful gloom that joy forbids,
        The mourners' silent tread,
The crypt, the coffin's stony lids,—
Sad as a soul the maze that thrids
Of dark Amenti, ere it rids
        Its way of judgment dread.

This glorious arch, these climbing towers,
        Are all for life and cheer !
Part of the new world's nobler dowers ;
        Hint of millenial year
That comes apace, though evil lowers,—
When loftier aims and larger powers
Will mould and deck this earth of ours,
        And heaven at length bring near !

Unmoved its cliffs shall crown the shore ;
  Its arch the chasm dare ;
Its network hang, the blue before,
  As gossamer in air ;
While in and out, forevermore,
The surging tides of ocean pour,
And past its towers the white gulls soar
  And winds the sea-clouds bear !

Heroes.

The winds that once the Argo bore
  Have died by Neptune's ruined shrines,
And her hull is the drift of the deep sea-floor,
  Though shaped of Pelion's tallest pines.
You may seek her crew on every isle
  Fair in the foam of Aegean seas,
But, out of their rest, no charm can wile
  Jason and Orpheus and Hercules.

And Priam's wail is heard no more
  By windy Ilion's sea-built walls ;
Nor great Achilles, stained with gore,
  Shouts, "O ye Gods ! 'tis Hector falls !"
On Ida's mount is the shining snow,
  But Jove has gone from its brow away,
And red on the plain the poppies grow
  Where the Greek and the Trojan fought that day.

235

Mother Earth! Are the heroes dead?
  Do they thrill the soul of the years no more?
Are the gleaming snows and the poppies red
  All that is left of the brave of yore?
Are there none to fight as Theseus fought
  Far in the young world's misty dawn?
Or to teach as gray-haired Nestor taught?
  Mother Earth! Are the heroes gone?

Gone? In a grander form they rise;
  Dead? We may clasp their hands in ours;
And catch the light of their clearer eyes,
  And wreathe their brows with immortal flowers.
Wherever a noble deed is done
  'Tis the pulse of a Hero's heart is stirred;
Wherever Right has a triumph won
  There are the Heroes' voices heard.

Their armor rings on a fairer field
  Than the Greek and the Trojan fiercely trod;
For Freedom's sword is the blade they wield,
  And the gleam above is the smile of God.
So, in his isle of calm delight,
  Jason may sleep the years away;
For the Heroes live, and the sky is bright,
  And the world is a braver world to-day.

Lizette Woodworth Reese.

[Of Baltimore, Maryland.   Her first volume " A Branch of May"
appeared in 1887.   "A Handful of Lavender" was issued four
years later   The poems selected are quoted by permission of the
author, and by special arrangement with her publishers, Houghton,
Mifflin & Co., Boston.]

A Haunting Memory.

Wild rockets blew along the lane ;
  The tall white gentians too were there ;
The mullein stalks were brave again ;
  Of blossoms was the bramble bare ;
    And toward the pasture bars below
    The cows went by me, tinkling slow.

Straight through the sunset flew a thrush,
  And sang the only song he knew,
Perched on a ripening elder bush ;
  (Oh, but to give his song its due !)
    Sang it, and ceased, and left it there
    To haunt bush, blade, and golden air.

Oh, but to make it plain to you !
  My words were wrought for grosser stuff ;
To give that lonely tune its due,
  Never a word is sweet enough ;
    A thing to think on when 'twas past,
    As is the first rose or the last.

The lad, driving his cows along,
　　Strode whistling through the windy grass ;
The little pool the shrubs among
　　Lay like a bit of yellow glass ;
　　　　A window in the farmhouse old,
　　　　Turned westward, was of glaring gold.

I have forgotten days and days,
　　And much well worth the holding fast ·
Yet not the look of those green ways,
　　The bramble with its bloom long past,
　　　　The tinkling cows, the scent, the hush—
　　　　Still on the elder sings that thrush.

Tell Me Some Way.

Oh, you who love me not, tell me some way
Whereby I may forget you for a space ;
Nay, clean forget you and your lovely face—
Yet well I know how vain this prayer I pray.
All weathers hold you. Can I make the May
Forbid her boughs blow white in every place ?
Or rob June of her rose that comes apace ?

Cheat of their charm the elder months and gray ?
Aye, were you dead, you could not be forgot :
So sparse the bloom along the lanes would be ;
Such sweetness out the briery hedges fled ;
My tears would fall that you had loved me not,
And bitterer tears that you had gone from me ;
Living, you break my heart, so would you dead !

———————

Rachel.

No days that dawn can match for her
   The days before her house was bare ;
Sweet was the whole year with the stir
   Of young feet on the stair.

Once she was wealthy with small cares,
   And small hands clinging to her knees ;
Now is she poor, and, weeping, bears
   Her strange, new hours of ease.

———————

April Weather.

Oh, hush, my heart, and take thine ease,
  For here is April weather !
The daffodils beneath the trees
  Are all a-row together.

The thrush is back with his old note ;
  The scarlet tulip blowing ;
And white—ay, white as my love's throat—
  The dogwood boughs are growing.

The lilac bush is sweet again ;
  Down every wind that passes,
Fly flakes from hedgerow and from lane ;
  The bees are in the grasses.

And Grief goes out, and Joy comes in,
  And Care is but a feather ;
And every lad his love can win,
  For here is April weather.

———————

Harriet Prescott Spofford.

[Born at Calais, Maine, 1835. Poet and novelist. The poem selected is quoted by permission of the author and by special arrangement with her publishers, Houghton, Mifflin & Co., Boston.]

The Lonely Grave.

Blood-red the roses blossom in the dell,
The bosky place where once the battle fell ;
Tall have the grasses grown since then, and rank
The ferns, fed with the ghastly dew they drank.
O sweet, sweet, sweet these roses of the South ;
Sweet these rain-lilies blowing after drouth ;
Sweet the wild grape, whose bunches everywhere
Fling spice upon the lonesome summer air ;
Sweet the great orange boughs and jasmine flowers
In dawn and dusk through all the visiting hours
That troop across the hidden grave's low swell
Where the palmetto stands, a sentinel !

A lonely grave,—none care for it, none know
His name who all these seasons sleeps below.
Only the heedless hunter pauses there
To sight some wing that quivers in the air,
Nor feels the presence of an ancient pain
That yearns about the unknown spot in vain.

Only the noonday sunshine comes ; the rain ;
The golden moons above it wax and wane ;
The wild deer crouch beside it, and the snake
Glitters and slips along beneath the brake ;
While, from the dagger-tree the bubbling song
Of mocking-birds makes music all night long.

But far on northern hills a woman grows
The sadder with each gust the south wind blows ;
A mother listens, and with eager ears
The step long hushed in every footfall hears ;
And friends, flower laden, in a martial rout
Among the fortunate graves go in and out.
Ah, if to-day one violet fell here,
One bluebell dropped its heaven-holding tear,
One homely door-stone blossom shed its breath,
Less desolate with the despair of death,
For all the song, the splendid glow and gleam,
This lush-leaved covert of the dead would seem !

Yet, on this sole day of the waiting year,
Since love with its dear tribute comes not near,
Its shadow steals through the green under-gloom
To scatter armfuls of pale myrtle bloom,—
A dark shape, crooning o'er the lonely grave,
The wildly-tuned thank-offering of the slave.

Harriet Prescott Spofford.

For here, where strange boughs move and strange wings
    whirr,
He rests upon his arms who died for her.
Brighter the tide that wet the soil returns,
And in the blaze of the pomegranate burns ;
Loftier the heavens climb from that low grave,
Tenderer the air to which his breath he gave.
Because he died, her children are her own ;
Her soul, she cries, to a white soul has grown ;
Because he sleeps beneath an alien sod
Her race in fuller sunlight answers God.
O sweet the bosky dell in sun and shower,
Sweet the low wind that creeps from flower to flower !
O sweet, sweet, sweet these roses of the South,
The breath of the rain-lilies' honeyed mouth ;
Sweet the bird's song across the lonely grave,
But sweeter still the blessings of the slave !

243

Stuart Sterne.

[This is the pen-name of Gertrude Bloede, born in Dresden, Germany, 1845. She came to America in 1850 with her parents, her father being a refugee from the revolutionary troubles of his native city. Since 1861 she has lived in Brooklyn, N.Y. The poems selected are quoted by permission of the author and by special arrangement with her publishers, Houghton, Mifflin & Co., Boston.]

Night After Night.

Night after night we dauntlessly embark
  On slumber's stream, in whose dark waves are drowned
  Sorrow and care, and with all senses bound,
Drift for a while beneath the sombre arc
Of that full circle made of light and dark
  Called life,—yet have no fear, and know refound
  Lost consciousness shall be, even at the sound
Of the first warble of some early lark,
Or touch of sunbeam.   Oh, and why not then
Lie down to our last sleep still trusting Him
Who guided us so oft through shadow dim,
Believing somewhere on our sense again
Some lark's sweet note, some golden beam shall break,
And with glad voices cry, " Awake ! Awake ! "

Compensation.

"Lord, I am weary!" cried my soul. "The sun
  Is fierce upon my path, and sore the weight
Of smarting burdens ; ere the goal be won
  I sink, unless thou help, dear Lord !" and straight
    My fainting heart rose bravely up, made strong
    To bear its cross : God granted me a song !

"Lord, I am conquered ! Ceaseless, night and day,
  A thousand cruel ills have hedged me round,
Till like a stag the hounds have brought to bay
  My stricken heart lies bleeding on the ground !"
    When lo ! with new-found life my soul, made strong,
    Spurned all its foes : God granted me a song !

"Lord, I am dying ! Earth and sea and sky
  Fade and grow dark ; yet, after all, the end
Wrings from my breaking heart a feeble sigh
  For this poor world, not overmuch its friend !"
    But suddenly with immortal power made strong
    My soul, set free, sprung heavenward in a song !

Celia Thaxter.

[Celia Laighton (Mrs. Thaxter) was born at Portsmouth, N.H., 1835. Died at the Isle of Shoals, 1894. The poems selected are quoted by special permission of Houghton, Mifflin & Co., Boston.]

The Sand-Piper.

Across the narrow beach we flit,
  One little sand-piper and I ;
And fast I gather, bit by bit,
  The scattered drift-wood, bleached and dry.
The wild waves reach their hands for it,
  The wild wind raves, the tide runs high,
As up and down the beach we flit,
  One little sand-piper and I.

Above our heads the sullen clouds
  Scud black and swift across the sky,
Like silent ghosts in misty shrouds
  Stand out the white light-houses nigh.
Almost as far as eye can reach,
  I see the close-reefed vessels fly,
As fast we flit along the beach
  One little sand-piper and I.

I watch him as he skims along,
  Uttering his sweet and mournful cry ;
He starts not at my fitful song,
  Or flash of fluttering drapery.
He has no thought of any wrong,
  He scans me with a fearless eye ;
Staunch friends are we, well-tried and strong,
  This little sand-piper and I.

Comrade, where wilt thou be to-night,
  When the world storm breaks furiously?
No drift-wood fire will burn so bright—
  To what warm shelter canst thou fly ?
I do not fear for thee, though wroth
  The tempest rushes through the sky ;
For are we not God's children both,
  Thou little sand-piper and I ?

O Tell Me Not.

O, tell me not of heavenly halls,
  Of streets of pearl and gates of gold,
Where angel unto angel calls
  'Mid splendors of the sky untold.

John Charter.

My homesick-heart would backward turn
   To find this dear, familiar earth,
To watch its sacred hearth-fires burn,
   To catch its songs of care or mirth.

I'd lean from out the heavenly choir
   To hear once more the red-cock crow,
What time the morning's rosy fire
   O'er hill and field began to glow.

To hear the ripple of the rain,
   The summer waves at ocean's brim,
To hear the sparrow sing again
   I'd quit the wide-eyed cherubim !

I care not what heaven's glories are !
   Content am I.   More joy it brings
To watch the dandelion's star
   Than mystic Saturn's golden rings.

And yet, and yet,—O dearest one,
   My comfort from life's earliest breath,
To follow thee where thou art gone,
   Through those dim, awful gates of Death,—

To find thee,—feel thy smile again,
   To have Eternity's long day
To tell my grateful love,—why, then,
   Both heaven and earth might pass away !

Edith Matilda Thomas.

[Born at Chatham, Ohio, 1854. The poems selected are quoted by the special permission of the author and the consent of her publishers, Houghton, Mifflin & Co., Boston.]

Augury.

I.

A horseshoe nailed, for luck, upon a mast :
That mast, wave-bleached, upon the shore was cast !
I saw, and thence no fetich I revered,
But safe, through tempest, to my haven steered.

II.

The place with rose and myrtle was o'ergrown,
Yet Feud and Sorrow held it for their own.
A garden then .I sowed without one fear,—
Sowed fennel, yet lived griefless all the year.

III.

Brave lines, long life, did my friend's hand display.
Not so mine own ; yet mine is quick to-day.
Once more in his I read Fate's idle jest,
Then fold it down forever on his breast.

On the Eve of Sleep.

What is softer than two snowflakes meeting
   In a windless fall of snow?
What is lighter than a down-ball sinking
   On a still stream's polished flow?
Smoother than the liquid circle spreading
   From the swallow's touch-and-go?—
Oh, softer, lighter, smoother, is the first approach of Sleep!
(Yet guard us in that moment, lest thy boon we may not keep!)

What is stiller than two blossoms kissing
   Charily with petal-tips?
Sweeter than the dewdrop that their kissing
   Doth unsphere—and down it slips?
What is dimmer than the night-moth groping
   For the lily's nectared lips?—
Oh, stiller, sweeter, dimmer, is the first approach of Sleep!
(Yet guard us in that moment, lest thy boon we may not keep!)

What is subtler than the clues that tighten
   Round the dancing midge's wings?
Shyer than the bird its nest concealing,
   As aloof it flits and sings?

Closer than the poppy-leaf-lined chamber
  Where the lone bee's cradle swings ?—
Oh, subtler, shyer, closer, is the first approach of Sleep !
(Yet guard us in that moment, ere we reach thy safest deep ')

What is stranger than the moonlight mingling
  With the red fire of the west ?
Wilder than an Amazonian forest
  Where no foot the mould hath pressed ?
Dearer than the heart's most secret brooding
  On the face it loveth best ?
Oh, stranger, wilder, dearer, is the first approach of Sleep !
(Oh, guard us in that moment, lest we waver back and weep!)

The Oread.

She dwells upon the fountained heights serene,
  I by the broadening river's sullied flow ;
  She could not breathe the air we breathe below,
Nor we the air that wraps her pure demesne.
Light loves her ; there the morning first is seen,
  There long delays the wistful afterglow ;
  Above her gleams the fountain-feeding snow,
Beneath are forests all the twelvemonth green.

She dwells afar ; yet still the river sings
  What she has sung above its cradle bright ;
I look, and lo ! the swarthy current brings
  An alpine bloom slipped through her fingers white ;
But not until the rivers seek their springs
  May any gift of mine achieve her height.

The Grasshopper.

Shuttle of the sunburnt grass,
Fifer in the dun cuirass,
Fifing shrilly in the morn,
Shrilly still, at eve unworn ;
Now to rear, now in the van,
Gayest of the elfin clan :—
Though I watch their rustling flight,
I can never guess aright
Where their lodging-places are ;
'Mid some daisy's golden star,
Or beneath a roofing leaf,
Or in fringes of a sheaf,

Edith Matilda Thomas.

Tenanted as soon as bound !
Loud thy reveille doth sound,
When the earth is laid asleep,
And her dreams are passing deep,
On mid-August afternoons ;
And through all the harvest moons—
Nights brimmed up with honeyed peace,
Thy gainsaying doth not cease !
When the frost comes, thou art dead—
We along the stubble tread,
On blue, frozen morns, and note
No least murmur is afloat ;
Wondrous still our fields are then,
Fifer of the elfin men !

———